Becoming James Cass

L.L. COLLING

Copyright © 2020 L.L. COLLING

www.pandamoniumpublishing.com

All rights reserved. No part of this book may be used or reproduced in any manner whatsoever without the prior written permission of the publisher, except in the case of brief quotations embodied in reviews. This book is a work of fiction. The characters, incidents, events, and dialogue are drawn from the author's imagination and are not to be constructed as real. Any resemblance to actual events or persons, living or dead, is entirely coincidental.

Cover design: Alex Goubar

ISBN: 978-1-989506-04-2

DEDICATION

To everyone who wonders if this story is about them, it is.
If you wanted me to write well of you, you should have behaved better.

www.pandamoniumpublishing.com

This book is the prequel to Obsessed with Her by L.L. Colling

Sometimes, I pray for you at night. Someday, maybe you'll see the light.

1

My life wasn't always this way. There's a place tucked deep in my mind of a splinter of time where I was still a decent human being. It seems so far away that I'm not sure if it's real or if it's a made-up memory. I've fallen far from where I was supposed to be in my life; away from the things that I thought I knew and the things that I was sure I believed. I don't know what I believe anymore. But one thing I do know…I'm not the person I want to be. No one would ever want to be the person I've become.

Tuesdays are typical; I say typical because I like that word better than predictable. I'm sitting around a poker table with a bunch of guys that I've known for what seems like forever, in the same chair, in the same backroom of Jimmy's deli. That's not the name of the place according to the sign on the building, but that's what we call it. It's hot as balls in here and I think the heat is starting to get to me.

"Isn't your A/C working, Jimmy? It's fucking hot in here and I'm about to lose my mind," I say as I push my sleeves up my arms. "My forearms are even starting to sweat."

Jimmy takes a drag on his cigar, raises and eyebrow, "It's been down for a couple of days, fuckin' guys can't figure out what's wrong with it. Have another drink and shut up about it…"

"So how do you keep the meat cold?" Tommy interrupts.

"Of course, you fat fuck would be worr...why don't you just let me handle my own business and you stay the fuck outta it, ok? It's not the refrigeration system, dummy, the meat is fine." Jimmy shakes his head and throws a couple hundred dollars of chips onto the middle of the table.

Tommy shrugs his shoulders and I place my bet. I put my finger in the air for another scotch and Jimmy's wife nods. Damn, Jimmy's wife; no wives are allowed here, but she's an exception and I'm glad. She sets down my drink and takes a long drag on her cigarette. I can imagine her lips puckered around something else. Her black skirt barely covers her ass and her boobs spill out of her sparkly, sleeveless top. She's got too much makeup on and in this heat, I'm surprised it's not melting down her face. I'm a sucker for red lipstick. I can't tell how many drinks I've already downed, but I can say it's enough to fell feeling warm and fuzzy and

"Jimmy, you almost done?" she asks.

"No, we'll go when I say we go...how many times do I have to tell ya?" He answers as he inspects his poker hand.

She rolls her eyes before disappearing into the back. I decide to follow her. I've been wanting to get her alone all night and now's my chance.

"I need to piss," I fold and get up from the table. Nobody looks up from their hand.

She's in the back hallway sitting on a chest freezer; she's picking at her nail polish as I squeeze by her.

"You're bored," I say with a smirk.

"Yeah," she smiles back without looking up at me. I glance down the hallway and check if the guys can see us from this angle. They can't.

"How come you're here every week? Jimmy won't leave you home alone?" I laugh.

I know for a fact that Jimmy treats her like shit. She's come in here more than enough times with her face bruised and a fat lip.

"He brings me here because he thinks I'll be bored at home by myself with nothing to do."

"I can think of something that would keep you busy," I say.

"Yeah?" She flips her hair over her shoulder and I'm about to explode if I can't stick it in her.

"Yeah," I breathe.

"I thought you said the last time that it was the *last time*…" she trails off as I bite her earlobe gently.

"I lied."

"Are you sure you want to do this? I mean, what about your wife?"

"She's not here last time I checked…have you seen her? She's not exactly…well…she's not you, let's put it that way."

I kiss her on the mouth; I never fucking liked Jimmy anyway, he's a piece of shit. I brush my hand against her knee, and she doesn't flinch, she doesn't say a word. She takes my hand and places it on the inside of her thigh. She smiles and slides my hand up to her crotch; she jumps off the freezer and takes me by the hand to the bathroom.

I'm ready- It doesn't take much. I lock the door behind me, and she jumps onto the bathroom counter. I kiss her because I'm a gentleman and I don't want to seem too eager, like I was last time when I thought my head was going to explode. She takes my face in her hands, I gently bite her neck, and she takes a deep breath while I peel off her panties.

She undoes my belt buckle and pulls it out. Her hands are icy, and I jerk back for a second.

"You're freezing," I whisper in her ear as I lick it.

"I know, my hands are always cold," she says.

"It's a thousand degrees in here!"

"My hands are always cold," she repeats.

I push inside of her. Thankfully that part of her is warm and my God does she feel good. She digs her nails into my back as I move harder and faster. I'm going to burst. It's a problem at this age, trying not to pop my cork too soon. There's a loud BANG outside in the hallway and it startles me for a second, but not enough to stop. All the sudden the door is kicked in and I'm caught with my pants down, inside of another man's wife.

Without finishing, I pull up my pants, and a cop says, "Wow Doc, I didn't expect this." He gestures to the situation. "Don't make me cuff you. Play nice."

"Can I at least do up my fly?" I ask.

"Yeah, hurry up," the cop says.

He brings me to the front of the deli. Jimmy, Vinnie, Charlie, Mike, Tommy, and I don't look at each other.

"Gentlemen," says the cop, "We have a big problem. We're responding to a noise complaint made earlier this evening."

We all stare at each other for a second and share knowing glances. They aren't here for a noise complaint. Here we go again.

"A noise complaint? Guys, can't you do better than that?"

"One of your neighbors called it in. Said that the noise was going on for hours and was becoming unbearable. She was trying to get her baby to sleep."

"We don't have any neighbors, none with kids especially. This entire block is zoned commercial. That's bullshit."

"Well, looks like it's our word against yours," the cop smiles at his partner as he nods.

Vinnie holds his finger up to his mouth and pauses as he taps his ear.

"Do you hear any fucking noise in here?" he asks.

"Yeah, it's deafening actually." The cop says with a raised eyebrow. He does not break Vinnie's stare.

"Gimme a fucking break! Why don't you go and arrest some *real* criminals? Make yourselves useful for a change," Vinnie practically spits.

I glance at Tommy and he smirks. I can tell he's trying to keep his mouth shut and I wonder how long he'll be able to. Tommy hates cops, everyone in our line of work does, but Tommy especially because his dad was killed by them in a shootout when Tommy was eleven years old. I shouldn't say *our* line of work because this is not at all what I do for a living. Charlie's eyes dart around the room and settle comfortably on the cop's face when he realizes that we've left no drugs or guns out in the open.

"Vinnie, you're not a *real* criminal? Do I need to remind you of your rap sheet? Want me to recite it from memory? How much time do you have? This could take a while."

"Fuck you," Vinnie says.

The cop looks at the poker table, "Where's all this money from? You're not breaking the law with illegal gambling are you, Vin?"

"What? Having money is against the law? It's only a few hundred dollars, probably more than you make though, right? Now I get it, that's what the *real* problem is." Vinnie raises an eyebrow for a split second, and I can read his mind. He's thinking, *if they only knew how much money was in the wall, we'd all be doing twenty years, not to mention the fifteen unregistered guns hidden throughout the place.*

"No illegal gambling going on here," Vinnie says ignoring the part about where the money was from.

"What did you say?" The cop asks and takes a step closer to him.

Vinnie holds his ground, "I said you're wrong. This is social gambling, a game among friends and is the furthest thing from illegal. It's poker night, that's all it is. You're reaching."

"Well it's a good thing that we responded to that noise complaint isn't it? Imagine our surprise when we respond to a noise complaint and find you guys around a poker table with a ton of cash and this one in the back with his pants down," The cop points to me. "Talk about hitting the jackpot!"

"Listen, when you gotta piss, you gotta piss," Vinnie says coming to my defence. "What? Is that illegal too?"

I look at Jimmy and he looks at his wife, I know by the look on his face that he knows what happened. She stares at the floor and I wonder how bad she's going to get it when they get home. Part of me feels bad, but another part doesn't; she knew exactly what the consequences would be. Thank god he didn't know about all the other times we were together though, or it may have been a different story and I'd be the one taking a shit kicking.

"You guys are in here every fucking week. And every week, there's nothing for you to charge us with. When the fuck will you learn that we're smarter than you? You think we're going to do illegal shit with you guys showing up out of the blue? Making up some weak excuse like a noise complaint to see if you can catch us in the act of doing whatever the fuck you think we're doing?"

"One of these days your luck is going to run out, Vin," the cop says. "And I'll be right there, ready to arrest you, finally. You've been too lucky for too long." Vinnie doesn't answer, and the cop continues to antagonize him, "We're going to have to issue you a ticket," he smirks.

"You can't ticket us. For what? For a fake noise complaint?" Mike says. "You could hear a pin drop in here."

"Actually, we can, and we are."

Mike shakes his head and swears under his breath in Italian. Tommy, Charlie, and I remain silent and let Vinnie and Mike handle things.

All eyes are on the cop as he scrawls some chicken scratch across a notepad.

"Are you done yet? How long does it take to write a ticket? Are you stalling? Are we going to sit here and hold hands and sing fucking Kumbaya all fucking night waiting for you to finish?" Vinnie asks.

"Vinnie, you'd better watch it. You're on thin ice already. It's only going to be a matter of time before I collar you for all the stupid shit you've done. And when that day comes, it's going to be one to celebrate.

The cop holds out the ticket and Vinnie snatches it from his hand, "Five hundred dollars? Are you fucking kidding me?"

"Is that too much?" The cop raises an eyebrow and points to the money on the table, "You look like you can afford it."

Vinnie doesn't speak but shakes his head in bewilderment.

"Have a nice night gentleman, and don't forget to pay your fine on time," the cop says as he and his partner exit the room.

There's silence for a beat before Charlie speaks, "Can you believe those fucking pigs? Comin' in here like they own the place thinkin' that they can do whatever the fuck they want without consequence. Just once I'd like to be alone with them one on one. I'd give them the beating of their life."

"Fuck them, don't worry about it. They're never going to catch us with our dicks in our hands, I'll tell ya that right now," Tommy says.

"I need another drink," Charlie says. He goes behind the counter and opens a brand-new bottle of whiskey, "Isn't this your job, sweetheart?" he says to Jimmy's wife. "I mean, why else do we keep you around?"

"Fuck you, Charlie," Jimmy's wife says.

"Hey, don't talk to him like that, have a little respect," Jimmy says to her.

She rolls her eyes and I almost laugh out loud at the irony.

"And get us some ice," he continues.

She does as she's told, and we hold out our glasses for her to fill them as she takes over the bottle from Charlie.

When she gets to me, she doesn't make eye contact. I can't tell if she's embarrassed about us being caught or upset that we didn't get to finish. Maybe she's worried about what's going to happen when Jimmy takes her home. He seems pretty chill about it, probably because it's happened with everyone around this poker table at least once. Me and her, more than once…more than a dozen times.

We play a couple more hands, throw our chips in, Tommy calls, and it's all over for me. At least I'm getting out of here with the shirt on my back. I'm on a losing streak, I don't know what it is, I've got a lot on my mind, I know that, but tonight for some reason I'm not able to focus. Maybe it's the five whiskeys.

"Let's call it a night," Vinnie says.

We all agree. I check my watch, it's just about 2:30 before we go our separate ways. I'm not near sober enough to be driving, but what choice do I have? I'm not about to call a cab and it's not like I live that far away. I keep telling myself this, so I don't feel like a scum bag, drinking and driving piece of shit.

Back when I had just graduated from University, long before I made a disaster of my life, I was working as an intern at a hospital. I finished my shift at seven in the morning and was walking home. A drunk driver slammed into a little girl and her mother as they crossed the intersection, and the kid died in my arms. I had night terrors for years after, but I never stopped drinking, I just stopped drinking and *driving*…for a while anyways. Drinking numbs the pain, and whoever thinks it doesn't, hasn't had enough to drink.

For me, it goes in phases, I have a couple of drinks and I feel pretty good, then I have a couple more and the memories start to come back. So, I have a few more to get rid of them and before I know it, I'm balls deep inside of some broad I've never met, and her husband is beating the shit out of me because he found us fucking in their shower. But that only happened twice that I can remember.

*

I don't know how I got home, probably that part of the brain that operates on autopilot, but I've reached my destination of the driveway. I throw the car into park and stumble onto the front porch. I didn't feel the booze this much before, but maybe it's because I just finished the last two sips from a bottle of gin under the front seat that I keep there for emergencies.

I laugh and then tell myself to be quiet as I shove my keys into the lock. Nope, that's not the keyhole, that's not it either as my key scratches the paint on the door. I stagger over to the porch swing and make a bed for myself out of a decorative pillow and a throw blanket, looks like I'll be spending the night out here. The door opens and the light flicks on, I can barely lift my head.

"Dad?"

"Yeah?"

"Are you ok?"

"Yes baby, I'm fine."

"You're planning on sleeping out here?" Emmie smirks.

"Yes, don't tell your mother."

"She's not home, she's at a school thing overnight, some conference…remember?"

"Really? Well that makes a difference, I would have pounded down the door for you to let me in! Who wants to sleep on a porch?"

"Come on, Daddy. I'll help you inside and up to bed."

"Why is your mother at school?"

"Dad, it's been on the calendar for a month. I don't know what her meeting is about, I have no idea. What I do know is that you need to come inside."

"Oh. I didn't realize what day it was…I mean I did, but now I don't know. I did know, but now I don't. Do you know what I mean? Does that ever happen to you?"

"Dad, you need to get to bed, ok? Let me help you."

"Thank you, Princess. Daddy loves you. You know that right?" I ask as I kiss her forehead while she helps me up from the swing.

"I know. Rough night at Poker again?"

"How did you guess?"

"Because it's Tuesday…we'll technically it's Wednesday, now."

I smile, "You're a good girl and I love you. I'll take you to school in the morning."

"It's summer, Dad, I don't have school tomorrow. You were at my graduation two weeks ago."

"Ok good, I'll make us pancakes."

"Make them in the morning, right now, you need to get some sleep, it's getting early."

I trip up the stairs once or twice on the way to my bed and I don't bother to take off my clothes. My daughter puts something on the nightstand and gives me a kiss on the cheek.

"Goodnight, Dad."

"Love you, sweetheart," I mutter and I'm out like a light.

2

The sun slaps me in the face and my head is splitting like a tree struck by lightning. My eyes squint and I wish that my wife would get some curtains that do *anything* more than the ones we currently have. She says they're for decoration and to let as much light in as possible. That sounds like the exact opposite of what curtains are supposed to do.

I roll over and check the alarm, it flashes 10:37. It feels like I've got a mouth full of cotton balls, so I'm grateful for the room temperature glass of water on the nightstand and the two aspirin beside it. My kid is a saint. I pop the aspirin into my mouth and accidentally crush one with my teeth; there can't be a worst taste in the entire world. I make a face and swish the water around in my mouth for a second to clear it of the chalky paste. Gross. I check my phone, no missed calls. Guess there are no changes to my schedule which I'm grateful for because I don't think I could drag my ass into work this early.

I shuffle to the bathroom and am happy that I didn't wake up in a puddle of my own piss. But I suppose that waking up in a puddle of *someone else's* piss would be much worse. I brush the taste of stale liquor, aspirin, and morning breath out of my mouth and splash some cold water on my face, I want to go back to bed, but I shouldn't. It would be nice to spend an entire day in bed, sleeping and watching tv, but it's only Wednesday I remind myself and I can't remember the last time I slept in. I peel off my clothes and chuck them into the corner, I'll just throw on my bathrobe.

No point in having a shower just yet or getting dressed since I don't have to be at work until seven tonight. Maybe I'll watch a movie or play online poker for a bit.

"Dad?" Emmie yells at me from the bottom of the staircase and breaks my train of thought.

"Yeah, honey?" I wish she would dial it down. I pinch the bridge of my nose and close my eyes. Yelling isn't helping my headache, so I go to the bannister.

"Your pancakes are on the counter; me and Audrey are out by the pool if you need us."

"Ok sweetheart, thank you," I say as I throw on my robe and descend the staircase to the kitchen. "Audrey? Who's Audrey?" She doesn't answer because she slams the patio door before I can get the words out.

My kid has a heart of gold, but she's a terrible cook, God help her. I examine the hard, dark brown disc and wonder if there's enough syrup in the world to save it…I don't think there is, it's like eating a hockey puck, though I'm sure I could get through that in less bites. But I'm a good dad so I choke it down after I drown the thing in sugar. I don't bother to use a fork and knife because there's no way a table saw could cut through this mess. I wash my hands, pour myself some orange juice and grab the paper off the counter before I head outside to the yard. Should I put on some clothes? Is it weird for a dad to be out at his pool in a bathrobe watching his teenage daughter and her friend swim? I'm not really watching them, and this is my house so I can do whatever I want, I decide.

I settle into my chair under the umbrella and put my glass on the table. I flip down my sunglasses from the top of my head before my corneas burst into flames and my hangover gets to level ten. I'd like to keep it at an eight if at all possible. I tighten the belt on my bathrobe and unfold the newspaper. I don't know why I bother to read this shit, it's so depressing. I guess it's just a habit. Headlines read, Death Toll Reaches Millions as Virus Rages On, and Man Dies in Police Custody. Fuck, I have to quit this. I chuck the paper to the side and return to my orange juice.

"How were your pancakes?" Emmie asks.

"They were perfect as usual," I lie through my teeth.

"You must have had different ones," a voice pipes up, and I have to stop myself from laughing. I peer over my sunglasses and raise an eyebrow.

"Dad, this is Audrey," Emmie says.

I get up from my chair and walk over to the loungers where they're painting their nails. Wow, this girl can't be eighteen or should I say, I hope she's eighteen, Jesus. I forget to breathe and stand there for a second.

"Hi," the girl says. She's got a body on her that's for sure, legs for days and a killer rack. Thank God I'm wearing sunglasses so she can't see what I'm looking at.

"Dad?" Emmie's voice breaks my concentration, "Are you going to say hi or just be weird and stand there?"

Damn. Am I being weird? I knew it, I knew I should have changed into something better than a bathrobe.

"Hi…what was your name again?" I ask.

"Audrey."

"Right. Hi Audrey."

She smiles one of those smiles that lets you know she's trouble. A smile like the Cheshire cat from Alice in Wonderland. Is this the same girl that Emmie told me about while I wasn't really listening last week when I drove her to the mall? My kid talks a mile a minute and sometimes I just zone out because she talks non-stop. I remember she said something about one of the girls in her class dating a teacher or screwing him or something. This girl looks like she would do that and that any man would let her.

"Dad?" Emmie says again.

"Yeah?"

"Are you ok?"

Emmie shoots me a glare that tells me I'm staring. What the fuck is wrong with me? I'm not twenty years old again, but I feel like I am, the way that I'm standing here drooling over tits and tan lines. Why do young women have to look *this way* at *this age*? It's not fair to the rest of us who are more than middle-aged and stuck in marriages we hate. At least I have another fantasy to call on when Gayle is lying there lifeless waiting for me to finish.

"I'm going to get some sunscreen, I forgot it on the kitchen counter," Emmie says as she moves to get up.

"I'll get it for you," I blurt. I have to get away from this girl, she's going to drive me fucking mental with the thought of what's under her bikini. I sure as fuck don't want to be alone with her out here.

"Thanks!"

I hurry to the kitchen and rub my face in my hands. *Snap out of it! She's the same age as your daughter for Christ's sake.* I rummage through the drawer in search of more aspirin and throw two more back with another glass of orange juice. The second glass tasted much better and less like that gross minty flavor after I just brushed my teeth. Are the only drinks we have in this house orange juice? Fuck! I don't know what else I want, but I'm sick of orange juice that's for sure. I hunt through the back of the fridge and navigate around energy drinks, protein shakes, and bottles of water, the patio door slams again, and I almost hit my head.

"Tell me what bills you pay to earn the right to slam doors in *my* house?" I say.

"Sorry! I didn't mean to slam it," A voice that is not Emmie's says.

Fuck. She's in my kitchen. Fuck, fuck, fuck, fuck, fuck, ahh, think of another word, shit.

    I remove my head from the fridge and smile. I try and look directly at her face as I'm not protected by sunglasses anymore, "Do you need something?" I stare at her face and don't blink. Did you know if someone stares at you for six seconds or more without blinking, they either want to kill you or they want to fuck you? I hope this girl doesn't know that tidbit of information.

    "Umm…Emmie was just wondering where the sunscreen is?"

    "Shit, sorry, I forgot. Here you go," I hand her the bottle.

    "Thanks."

Oh my God, please leave, please leave, please leave, I keep repeating this in my head over and over again, but she just stands there. She's smiling and I'm not entirely sure what my face is doing.

    "Is there something else you need?" I ask.

    "Well, I was just wondering if you could put some on my shoulders before I go out, they're already starting to burn."

I stand there like an asshole. My feet are cemented into the ground. *Think of something else, think of anything, think of your…I don't know, think of golf. Good, keep thinking of golf,* my brain commands. I picture the green, the clubs, the golf cart.

    "No, sorry. I absolutely can't do that."

She comes closer. She smells like coconut and rum. Now she's inches away from my face and she rubs a finger up my forearm. Goosebumps cover my body. This girl is electric.

    "Please?"

    I swallow hard, "No."

"Please? I never use the right amount. I could really use your help."

"I can't."

"Aww, how come?" she whispers as she touches my hand.

I jerk my hand away and say the first thing that comes to mind.

"I have an allergy to sunscreen so I can't touch it, or my skin will develop these…blisters and I could possibly go blind from it and…Emmie, thank God you're here!" I say as Emmie enters the room, saving my life. "Your friend Adrian, she needs uh, something, I don't know what she needs, she wants you to…"

"Dad, her name is Audrey…is everything ok in here?" Emmie smiles.

"Yes, yep!" I think I'm having a stroke.

"How many people does it take to get a bottle of sunscreen?" she shakes her head.

"Come on, Audrey the sun is in perfect position for us to bake. I took a bottle of wine out of the chiller, but it's starting to sweat. I refuse to drink warm wine, so let's go!"

Audrey shoots me a smile and simulates a blow job motion while Emmie has her back turned. They head back out to the pool. My eyes widen and I'm speechless; did I just imagine that, or did it happen? Did I hallucinate? Am I still drunk? I exhale and put both hands on the kitchen island. Holy fuck. I feel like I'm going to pass out. My legs feel like static on a television screen. I need a shower. A cold one.

*

The house is empty except for me and online poker. I skip the shower for now, I don't care if I smell. Emmie and her friend have left, thank god, and the color of my balls has been restored to normal. I push the thought of the girl out of my mind for now, I have to concentrate. Gayle won't be back for another hour which should be plenty of time for me to take these guys to task. She hates that I gamble and years ago she found out that I had spent almost thirty grand in a year on online slots and poker games. It sounds like a lot of money, but it's not. It was a thousand bucks here and there...well, almost every week I guess, and it slipped through my hands faster than I noticed. That was around the same time that she found secret text messages and phone calls to a couple of women I had got involved with sexually. It started off as friendship but turned X-rated pretty quickly.

To this day I never admitted to Gayle what I did with them, but in her heart, she knew, she'd be an idiot not to. I've been good at manipulating her, making her question her sanity at times, by telling her she's crazy and that I only have eyes for her. The truth is, I've been unhappy for as long as I can remember. Gayle used to be attractive at one point, but those days are long gone. She's let herself go. The other night when I was watching tv a show came on with a super sexy actress while Gayle was folding laundry in her bathrobe. I guess I was feeling ballsy because I said to her, "You don't even try anymore. You've given up." She cried and threw the laundry at me and went to bed. I slept in the guest room for a few nights, but I didn't care because it was the truth.

FUCK! I'm out. Down seven-hundred bucks just like that. I stare at the screen and watch as a player with the screen name *BBQTIME* bluffs his way to the top and takes the pot. Damn guy has been doing that all afternoon! I slam down the lid to my laptop and shake my head. Guess I should hit the shower. Gayle will be home any second.

*

The cold water washes over me, and it takes my breath away; I stand there for a few seconds until my thoughts swirl down the drain. I turn on the hot water and am finally satisfied with the perfect temperature. I lean my head back and take a deep breath in. The fogginess finally disappears from my brain. I've got to start thinking straight and I need my head securely fastened to my shoulders if I'm going to resolve anything. I've got problems. Big ones. I scrub my hair and five o'clock shadow with some sort of bar thing that Emmie says is going to save the world. It's a little disc of shampoo which resembles a bar of soap and there's no container. It smells like honey. I'm probably not using it right because I wash my whole body with it. Emmie always asks why I use them up so quickly, I tell her I don't know.

I rinse and dry off. I hear raised voices from downstairs. It's Gayle. Shit, I forgot to ask Emmie where she went. I throw on some clothes and go down to the kitchen as I say a quick prayer that Emmie's friend is gone and I'm relieved when I see that she is. That's one more thing that I don't need to deal with.

"Hi sweetie, how was your trip?" I ask and lean in for a peck on the cheek.

"James, I found *this* in *your* daughter's room," Gayle says as she holds up a joint.

I raise an eyebrow to my daughter who is only mine when there's a problem according to my wife. Emmie rolls her eyes and I want to do the same, it's joint for fuck's sake, not heroin or cocaine or even condoms or birth control, *that* would be something that I'd lose my shit over. I take the marijuana from Gayle and put it in the front pocket of my shirt.

"Why are you making such a big deal of this?" Emmie says and folds her arms.

"It's a big deal because you've brought drugs into this house! I'm not going to have drugs in my home, and you are NOT going to jeopardize your future by becoming a pothead! Marijuana is a gateway drug and leads to harder drugs!" Gayle says.

I want to laugh out loud, but I know better. I want to say to her that the worst thing that marijuana will do to our daughter is make her raid the fridge at two in the morning because she has the munchies, then she'll get a good sleep, and feel a bit thirsty the next day, not a big deal. There's no arguing with Gayle who thinks she knows everything after years of working in the public-school system and seeing all the *derelicts* as she calls them.

"Are you going to just stand there, James? Your daughter is headed down a dangerous path!"

"Gayle, you're overreacting…"

"See?" Emmie interrupts.

"James!" My wife yells.

"Emmie, that's not what I meant. You shouldn't be smoking pot, you know better. Gayle, she's *not* an addict, not even *close*, and she's a good…"

"I wished I had already smoked it because then you wouldn't have found it! What were you doing in my room anyway! Violating my privacy that's what!" Emmie interrupts.

Gayle's mouth is hanging open and it's amusing to me that my kid thinks that she's entitled to any privacy when she lives under my roof, rent free.

"Dammit, James! You're going to just stand there and take her side while I'm over here being the bad guy?"

"No, I just…" I say as my turn to speak is hijacked by two angry women. The hormones in this place are unreal and I don't know how I'm still living.

"This place is a prison! I can't do anything!" Emmie screams as she stomps down the hallway and grabs her keys off the table.

"This conversation is not over! Don't you walk away from me, little girl!" Gayle threatens as she follows her into the hallway.

"I'M NOT A LITTLE GIRL!" Emmie screams and slams the front door.

Gayle takes one look at me and shakes her head, "We're supposed to be a team, James. And you just stand there as usual with a stupid look on your face."

Her lecture was shorter and went better than I expected. I don't move as I feel like a deer being hunted. One wrong step and I'll be dead.

Gayle throws her hands in the air, "I'm going to the salon; now I'm late for my appointment!" I watch as she grabs her purse and keys from the bowl and pulls out of the driveway.

I pull the joint out of my pocket, sniff it, and search for a lighter. I'll smoke this by the pool later; it's just what I need to relax.

3

"Dad? Daddy?"

"Huh?" I yawn. *Where am I?*

"Dad, I'm going to Steph's tonight and staying over. I can't deal with mom, she's always in my face."

I'm groggy, "How long have I been asleep?"

"I don't know, Dad. I just got here."

"Where have you been?"

"I went for a drive and then I stopped at Audrey's to return her cell phone. She forgot it on the deck chair."

Images of the girl in her white bikini come flooding back and I have to shove them out of my mind quickly.

"Dad? What was going on with you guys in the kitchen? You were being so weird and acting strange. She didn't come on to you or anything did she?"

"Huh? No. What are you talking about? No. She was…she was just asking me where the sunscreen was."

"Are you sure? She's my friend and everything, but I mean, she did sleep with Mr. Larson, who is married with four kids by the way."

"What does that have to do with anything?" I pause. Shit.

"What does *that* have to do with *anything*? Dad, Mr. Larson cheated on his wife with Audrey, don't you think that's a big deal? She's a student, he's a teacher…what if I did that?"

"Watch your mouth; I don't ever want to hear you say that again. Talking about screwing around with your teacher…or any guy, married or otherwise for that matter. I raised you better than that!" I'm wide awake now.

"Dad, I'm not having sex with my teachers ok? But it's not like I haven't had sex before…remember Austin?"

"Oh my god! Why are we talking about this? And you mean to tell me that you guys had sex? I liked that kid…now he's a dead man if I ever see him again! Why are you telling me this now?"

"Because I knew that this would be your reaction!"

I cup my face in my hands, this is every father's worst nightmare, father's with daughters that is.

"Can we please not talk about this anymore? And please tell me that it was not in my house, under my roof."

"No, it was during spring break in Cozumel."

"Oh my god," I shake my head. "Sweetheart, I didn't pay for you to go on spring break to lose your virginity."

"Dad, it wasn't the first time or anything."

I sit there with my mouth gaping open, totally speechless.

"Enough. I don't ever want to have this conversation again. How many people have you been with exactly?"

"Are you sure you want to know?"

"Am I sure I want to…you've got to be kidding me…what kind of question is that? Let's just leave it at one so that I don't have a heart attack, ok?"

"Sure, Daddy. I'm going to Steph's. See you later." She gives me a kiss on the cheek.

"Ok, Emmie?"

"Yes?"

"Please make good choices."

"I will," she says and rolls her eyes.

"Have fun and no more weed today, promise me."

"I promise."

"Call me if you need anything."

"Thanks, Dad."

"And be good."

"Why do you always have to say that? I thought that you were the only person who understands me! I'm not a bad kid so why does mom have to be such a bitch?"

"Watch it, missy. She's still your mother and I don't want to hear you say that about her. She overreacted, but she loves you. You know how she gets with the whole you being our *miracle baby* and all."

"Just because you guys could only have one kid, doesn't make me a miracle. I honestly wished for a sibling my entire life because then I wouldn't always be the one with the attention thrown on me, or be the only one fighting with you guys because then, at least there would be some level of fairness, but I take the entire brunt of everything!"

I pause because I feel like I've taken a knife to the gut.

"Don't you think that your mother and I wanted more kids? Of course, we did! Don't you think it's a bit harsh for you to blame us for you not having a sibling? Emmie, we would have had more children if your mother was able and trust me when I say it killed her inside for a long time that we struggled with getting pregnant. But then you came along, and everything changed. We love you, Emmie."

"Sorry. She just makes me so mad! Everyone smokes pot! It's not like I'm shooting heroin or anything…"

"I know, sweetheart, trust me, I know."

"Can I have my joint back?"

"Absolutely not."

She shoots me a knowing look and I roll over to the other side of the lounge chair to get some more shut eye. Surprisingly the dope was quite good for being bought in a parking lot behind the mall from some raggedy ass teenager.

My phone rings, it's Gayle and I put her on speaker phone.

"Is Emmie home?"

Emmie shakes her head, rolls her eyes, and makes the cut sign across her neck.

"No, she just left."

"Ok, I'm coming home, they gave my appointment away…unbelievable."

"Ok, sweetheart. See you when you get here."

I hang up, "Well princess, you have about fifteen minutes to get your stuff packed and out of here before your mom comes home. I can't take much more of either of you."

"Thanks, dad!" My daughter says sarcastically before she runs into the house.

*

"Where is Emmie?"

"What, no "*hello*"? No "*sorry about what just happened*"?"

"I'm not sorry about what happened, our daughter..."

I interrupt her, "If this is the conversation we're having, I'm going inside. Enough, please."

Gayle sighs and resigns herself to doing as I say. I change the subject.

"How was your trip? I didn't get to ask you since you just barged in and started yelling."

She rolls her eyes, "It wasn't a luxury vacation so don't make it sound that way. It was the same as every other meeting. And for the record, I didn't just barge in and start yelling."

There's a silence and I brace myself for what's coming.

"You have no idea where I've been do you?"

And there it is.

"Of course, I do," I rack my brain for every possible idea of where Gayle may have been.

"Ok then, where was I?"

I take a shot in the dark and hope for the best, "You were at your teacher's thing."

"My *teacher's thing*? Really, James? I've been at a union meeting talking about...you know what? I've been a teacher for twenty-five... and...never mind, it doesn't matter. I don't expect you to know what I do, it's fine."

"You're a teacher, I know what you do! Jesus! Why do you have to turn everything I say into a fight?"

"I'm not fighting with you!"

"Yes, you are! You fight with me, you fight with Emm…"

My phone rings. It's the hospital. I stare at Gayle for a second as if waiting for her permission to pick it up.

"Answer it!" She says.

I get up from the lounger and answer the phone, "Yeah it's James."

"James, you working today?" Vinnie asks.

"Yeah, I'm going in to do some paperwork in about an hour."

"I'll meet you."

"Sure. Everything ok?"

"Yeah, I just want to talk."

My heart drops. What the hell did he want to talk about? I'm silent for a beat.

"You there?"

"Yeah, I'll leave now, see you in twenty minutes," I say, and I hang up the phone.

Gayle glares at me and I take a deep breath, "Listen to me, right now I have to go, but I promise that later, you and me will sit down and we'll talk about what to do with Emmie. We'll talk about everything, ok?"

"Fine." She spits.

"Are you ok? You look a bit grey in the face."

"Thanks."

"Sweetie, I'm just making sure you're ok. Are you feeling alright?"

"I'm fine! James, I'm just tired and stressed with Emmie and her going to school, and the drugs I found in her room…I'm fine, ok? You're going to be late."

I take a breath, "Ok, I'll see you tonight." I give her a kiss and head into the house to get changed.

*

I swipe my electronic key card and the door to my office unlocks. I press the button on the phone and Doris answers.

"Send him in."

"Sure, Doctor Cass, I'll send him in now."

My stomach swims when I hear footsteps in the hallway right outside of the door. The door swings open and it's Doris with Vinnie in tow.

"Thanks, Doris," I dismiss her.

I offer Vinnie a seat in the chair across from me and I take the seat behind the desk.

"Everything ok?" I ask.

"Yeah, everything is ok."

We sit in silence for a moment and I'm sure that he can hear my heart thudding against my ribcage.

"You're probably wondering why I'm here."

I smile. He's fucking with me.

"Vinnie, you know you're welcome here anytime, no invitation necessary."

"There are ten thousand places I'd rather be than in a fucking hospital…no offence." He says as he looks around the room at the cream-colored walls and framed certificates.

"None taken." I wish he would get to the point.

"I'm here because I thought you should hear this from me…in person."

My heart drops to my feet. I slowly move my hands to my knees and keep them there for a second to steady them.

"Jimmy is dead."

"What? How?"

"Couldn't keep his mouth shut so now he's at the bottom of the river."

"Us?"

"No."

"Fuck."

"Cops dragged his carcass out of there this morning, after receiving a tip from a truck driver who saw the whole thing. Might take a while for the cops to ID him though, since Tony Capelli cut his fucking head off."

"Jesus."

"Yeah."

"Why did they cut his head off?"

"Because he was fucking Tony Capelli's daughter. Tony caught Jimmy red handed, *in the act* if you know what I mean."

"Tony Capelli's daughter? What is he crazy? *Was* he crazy, I mean?"

"You would think he'd know enough to stay away, but then again; Jimmy was as dumb as fuck."

"What about the deli?" I ask.

"Nothing will change. It our club house, Jimmy just used it as a front to launder money for us. Now Tommy will take care of that."

"What about Jimmy's wife?"

"She hasn't said a word. She's a good girl. She knows the score." He takes another drink and smiles, "I know you were fucking her, shit most everyone was. She wasn't loyal to him, but could you blame her, the way he treated her? Busting her face once a week and slapping her around. I don't know how she put up with that shit and I'm surprised it wasn't her who killed him."

"Yeah, for sure," I say without a twinge of guilt for being included among the crowd that was sleeping with her.

"Leave her alone, James. I'm telling you. It's for your own good."

"I know, Vinnie. I was just thinking about her, I mean with Jimmy being dead and all…" I trail off.

"He got what was coming to him. But yeah, she's fine, I mean, what did you expect, but his mother is hysterical, calling everyone she knows to tell them that this was because of the shit he was into…do you have a glass of water?"

"Yeah, sorry! Let me get you one, where the fuck are my manners, Vinnie, I apologize," I say as I fumble to fill a disposable cup from the watercooler. I hand him the cup.

"Calm down, kid, it's fine. It's dry in here, ya know? I can't seem to get enough water throughout the day. Coffee and alcohol, I gotta cut that shit out. It's too much," he says between slurps.

"Yeah, you gotta take care of yourself, Vinnie."

"You sound like my wife."

"Sorry," I smile.

"Jimmy's mother is causing a huge problem for all of us, so don't be surprised if the cops come crawling in here asking questions about what you know."

"I'll be ready."

"You know what this mean, James?"

"Yeah…I know what it means." The hit on Jimmy from a rival gang meant war.

"Anything else?"

"No."

"Ok, I'll be in touch…we may need your services tonight, I'm not sure yet."

"Anything you need, Vin."

"Good." He stands up, shakes my hand, and leaves the room with the door open behind him.

I shut the door and lean my head against the glass; I can't believe Jimmy is dead. I mean I can believe it, no one deserved it more than that shit talking, troublemaking, dickhead, but still…If he was dead, that means it could happen to any one of us at any time. I pour myself a glass of water and turn on my computer. I can't concentrate. I have a ton of paperwork to catch up on, but all I can think about is Jimmy's mother. I'd met her once before, while stitching up one of Vinnie's drivers, at her kitchen table in the middle of the night. She was a tiny old lady, dressed in black all the time, but you could tell that she'd beat the shit out of you with her shoe, or a wooden spoon, or whatever was within reach if you did something she didn't like. The guy's face needed a bunch of stitches, because if I remember correctly, he took a set of brass knuckles to the forehead. Head injuries always look worse than they are, he bled a ton. The whole situation was so fucked up. While I was stitching the guy up, Jimmy's mother was making eggplant parmesan. She spoke only in Italian and kept shouting and waving her hands as she cooked. Jimmy was getting shit and we knew it. Now he's dead. Fuck.

I need to get out of here for a couple of hours. I'm not getting anything done and I need to let off some steam. I know where I'll go. I punch her number into my phone and tell her to meet me at our usual place in an hour. She agrees and I disconnect.

Then, I buzz my secretary in. She stands in the doorway waiting for my instructions.

"Doris, listen. Cancel all my consultations for tonight. Move them to later in the week. I've got a family situation to deal with and it needs my immediate attention."

"Everything ok, Doc?"

"Yeah, as ok as it can be."

"You don't have anything on your agenda for today, today was a *paperwork catch up day* as you put it. You have no consultations booked and no meetings." Doris straightens her glasses and looks up from her agenda. Why this woman won't go totally digital is beyond me. Sure, she uses the admin program on the computer, but she's never without her trusty day timer and pen. I guess on one hand it's a good idea to have an old school back up for just in case situations.

"Ok, well if there's nothing on my calendar for today, I'm going to work from home."

"Let me know if there's anything you need. Actually, you're going to need these files," she says as she hands me a memory stick. "Let me know if you have any problems accessing them."

"Doris, what would I do without you?"

"I don't know. Oh, and I ordered Mrs. Cass's birthday bouquet. It will be sent tomorrow."

"You ordered what?"

"Mrs. Cass's birthday is tomorrow," Doris says with a smile.

"Yes, ok well, good. Thank you for getting to that before I had a chance." We both know that I'm full of shit and that I forgot, and in fact I forget every year.

"My pleasure, sir," Doris says.

"What did we..."

She cuts me off, "I ordered the same thing as last year."

I stand there blankly, hoping that she'll save me the embarrassment of asking what she ordered last year.

"Thirty-six long stem roses."

"Yes, of course. Ok. That's perfect."

"It's a bit boring and generic, don't you think?"

I'm shocked that Doris is speaking so freely, she's never expressed her opinion in this way before.

"What do you mean? Women love roses, don't they?"

"Sure, for the most part."

"Doris, I'm in a bit of a rush, will you please get to the point and stop beating around the bush?"

"I'm just saying that red roses are the easy way out. There's absolutely no effort or thought put into that type of bouquet. It's almost as if this type of arrangement says, *"Here are some flowers that I don't care about, enjoy."* I mean, yeah they look pretty, but they're lazy in terms of romance."

"Thank you for your opinion, Doris. If this bothered you so much, then why did you order them?"

"Because Mrs. Cass isn't my wife. She's yours."

I smile and blink quickly a couple of times, "You ordered yourself something too, didn't you Doris?"

"Of course, I did, Dr. Cass. I saved you the embarrassment of forgetting my birthday which is next Wednesday."

I smile, "Good, thank you, Doris. Happy Birthday."

"Thank you, sir."

I shake my head and chuckle, "I don't know what I'd do without you."

"I know, sir. You'd be lost without me," Doris says. "Is that all you need?"

"Yes, that will be all, thank you."

She leaves the room and I grab my jacket off the coat rack and log out of my computer. I throw the memory stick into my briefcase and fish around for my keys. *Where the hell are they?*

I buzz Doris again and before I can get the words out, she says, "Inside, upper left jacket pocket."

"Thank you, Doris."

I lock my office door behind me and head to the parking lot. Thoughts of Jimmy swirl through my brain and I wonder what is going to happen and when in terms of retaliation. I know it's not my concern as I'm not a full-fledged member because of my non-Italian heritage, but Vinnie did say he would keep in touch and would call me when he needed me. I don't know what that means, and I could spend the rest of the day trying to figure it out, but right now, I've only got one thing on my mind.

I throw my briefcase on the passenger's seat and notice the pack of cigarettes calling my name. "Dammit, Emmie!" I breathe. I'm too lax with that kid, I should have made more rules and been stricter. If I had, she wouldn't be drinking wine all afternoon by the pool, smoking cigarettes and weed, and having sex. I push the thought of that out of my mind and focus on the task at hand. Get to the meeting place and get the release that I need.

4

I pull into the parking garage and look around. I need to make sure I'm not followed. Gayle hired a private investigator a couple of years ago and they produced her with enough proof of my infidelity that she could have taken Emmie and half of everything we owned. But no matter the evidence against me, she still wouldn't leave. She wanted us to go to counselling which of course, I refused. I thought it was a waste of my time and I'm not the type to explore my feelings or put the work into saving my marriage. I didn't give a shit if it ended or not, I was way past that point years ago. If she wanted to be stay married so badly, she would need to figure it out on her own. Why should I be the one to change? She could have left me a million times for a million different reasons, but she didn't. She decided to stay knowing exactly who I was and what I was like. I do another quick visual sweep and decide it's all clear. I grab my briefcase off the seat and finish my cigarette before I head through the front doors of the hotel.

"Hi, checking in," I say to the blonde behind the desk.

"Of course, sir. May I please have your last name?" Her hands hover over the keyboard.

"Thompson. I just made a reservation a few hours ago."

Within a few clicks she finds me, "Yes, I see you here. Thank you, sir. How long will you be staying with us?"

"Just for a couple of hours. I'm between flights as usual and my plane has a five-hour layover."

"I understand, sir," the blonde smiles at me and I smile back.

It's amazing how a briefcase and a five-thousand-dollar suit help with credibility. No one expects that I'm going to meet an escort, because when you dress respectable, you get respect. I don't like the word prostitute, it sounds dirty. Escort is high class, it's an experience and worth the price. Plus, I get to see the same one that I always do.

The woman finishes up on the computer and hands me the room key, "You're in room four-forty-sixty on the forty-second floor. Enjoy your stay!"

"Thank you, I'm sure I will," I say as I take the key and head to the elevator.

I check my reflection in the elevator mirror, straighten my tie, and adjust the bottom button on my three-piece suit. Whoever said a suit makes the man wasn't lying, I look like a million bucks. I step off the elevator and fob my way into the room. The stress from my conversation with Vinnie has all but disappeared. I text her the room number and pour myself a drink from the minibar. I take off my jacket and hang it on the back of a chair. My phone rings, it's Gayle; I can't think about her right now, so I decline the call. I wouldn't have to do what I'm doing if she just did what I wanted.

I take off my shoes and place them in the closet. All there is to do now is wait. I think about Jimmy again. I think about the mess that I'm in and how I got mixed up with Vinnie and the boys. Vinnie and I go way back, well, sort of. Our families go way back, and I've known him since I was fifteen years old. I guess I should say that I knew *of* him. My deadbeat, alcoholic father and I went toe to toe one night and I left the house and never came back. Jimmy was the one who introduced us because he was running errands for Vinnie and took me to meet him for the first time.

But, before I could get in tight with them, my aunt took me in as her own and set me on the straight and narrow, we moved to Cincinnati. She enrolled me into private school and then medical school. When I finished getting my degree, I did my internship in California because I wanted to return to my roots. I came back, Jimmy invited me to a poker game, and I lost my shirt. In the last year I personally owe Vinnie one hundred and fifty grand from gambling debts.

There's a knock on the door that snaps me back to reality and I check the peephole. It's her. I let her in, and she smiles.

"Hi."

"Hi, thanks for meeting me."

"Of course. Anything for you, James. You're my favorite customer."

"I know you say that to all of us."

She ignores me and takes off her coat. She looks good; a tight, black skirt with a hint of fishnets peeking out from underneath, above the knee leather boots, and a lace top. But she has to look good; she wouldn't be able to charge what she does if she didn't. I pass her a drink and sit beside her on the bed. I'm not sure if she can feel my uneasiness and I don't know why I'm feeling so nervous.

"So, were you looking for the usual thing?"

"I don't know what I'm looking for to be honest…"

"Ok honey, you just let me know what you like. I do it all. It's gonna be extra for that though if you know what I mean."

I nod, "No, I don't want anything extra."

"You seem stressed, honey."

"Maybe a little."

She rubs the inside of my leg and smiles, "Let me take your mind off things."

She moves her hand to my belt which she unfastens.

"Wait, can we just…" I breathe.

"Do you have a special request; did you change your mind? Whatever you want, honey," she whispers in my ear as she gently bites the lobe.

"I want to talk first…maybe just for a little while."

"Honey, you don't pay me to talk," she smiles, "How about you talk, and I relax you?"

She's right. I don't pay her to talk; I shut my mouth, lay back, and let her do the work.

*

I stare at her as she gets dressed; sexy women fascinate me, there is something magical about them, how soft they are, how good they smell, how they manage to walk in heels. I don't know how they do what they do, but it's hypnotic. I could stare at her all day long. She looks over her shoulder as she puts her stockings back on.

"Did you enjoy yourself?"

"What do you think? I'm pretty sure my reaction was obvious. Not like I can fake it."

She smiles, "Good, so did I."

Now I know she's lying. I get up from the bed and grab my wallet. I take out ten, crisp, hundred-dollar bills and place them on the dresser. Quality is important and you get what you pay for, safety is just as important, and I don't want to be bringing shit home or have sores all over my dick.

She takes the money and before she leaves says, "Call me any time ok? You're one of the good ones."

She kisses me on the cheek and disappears into the hallway; I'm alone with her words hanging in the air. *One of the good ones.* No, good guys don't hire prostitutes, they don't cheat on their wives, and they don't fall in deep with the wrong people. I'm the opposite of a good guy. A sliver of shame creeps up in me, but I push it down like I always do. Men are funny, most of us equate sex with love, but it's so much more than that; love is, fasten your seatbelt, have you eaten, take a sweater…those kinds of things. Just because someone doesn't love you the way that you think they should, doesn't mean that they don't love you with all they have.

The problem with love is that we all have this fucked up picture in our heads of what it should look like instead of seeing it the way it is. Ironically, It's the things we love the most that destroy us. Who am I to say what love is? I'm better versed in what it isn't. My thoughts turn to Gayle again, I don't know what's wrong with me today. I barely ever think of her, but for some reason she's on my mind. I think of all the shit she's put up with over the years because of my actions. She's the only person I know who would stay with someone who tried their best to get rid of them. It's not that I don't love her. Love is such a filthy word, I guess I don't respect her. If I did, I wouldn't lie or cheat or gamble or drink or do all the things that I do that hurt her. But the truth is, it's her fault for staying and not having a backbone.

She should have told me to fuck off years ago…maybe then I could respect her. She lets me walk all over her. I threaten to leave, and she begs me to stay. I don't know why she's stayed with me for as long as she has. She deserves someone better, someone who actually loves her. Sometimes I feel truly sorry for the way that I've treated her. And other times…I don't feel anything. One thing she always told me was *a mistake repeated, is a choice* and I made my choices that's for sure. I take another drink and quickly rinse off in the shower. I finish putting on my clothes, straighten my tie, and shut the door and my thoughts behind me; it's time to go home. I've had enough thinking for one day.

*

I sit in the driveway trying to compose myself before I go into the house. I spray myself with a bit of cologne, nothing overkill as not to be obvious that I'm trying to cover anything up and the rinse in the hotel shower washed her scent off of me; I pop a couple of pieces of gum into my mouth and check my face in the rearview mirror. I see Gayle's car in the driveway, and I have instant anxiety. What if she called the office looking for me and I wasn't there, what was I going to tell her? I needed a plan to answer her. If she asks me where I was, I'll tell her that I stepped out of the office to run an errand because it's her birthday tomorrow. Yes, perfect! She can't be mad at that. I wish Emmie were home because she cuts the tension between us. I hesitate again before going in and then finally get out of the car and step through the front door. I put my keys in the bowl and brace myself for Gayle's potential interrogation.

"What's going on here?" I ask when I see my daughter and my wife sitting together on the living room couch.

"What do you mean?"

"What do I mean? Are you *kidding me*? Earlier today you guys were at each other's throats and then the next second you're snuggled up together under a blanket.

"So?" Emmie says between mouthfuls of popcorn.

"The constant fluctuation of hormones in this house are going to be the death of me," I say.

"You're so dramatic!" she says.

"Aren't you supposed to be at your friend's house?"

"Yeah, I ended up coming home because I felt like sleeping in my own bed, plus Stephanie really annoyed me when she invited her boyfriend over and spent most of her time making out with him. I mean, I get it, he's pretty cute, but it was supposed to be girl's night."

I roll my eyes and sit beside Emmie. I wrap my arm around her and give her a kiss on the head.

"What are we watching?" I ask.

"Shh…Dad!"

"Ok, sorry!"

Gayle shoots me a smirk and passes me the popcorn just as my phone rings, it's Vincent. I get up from the couch and walk into the dining room.

"Hey Vin, what's up?"

"Just wanted to tell ya that Jimmy's funeral is tomorrow."

"What time?"

"Eleven at St. Stephen's."

"I'll see you then."

I hang up the phone and take a deep breath. Emotions will be running high and the guys will be on watch for other families; they'll be watching for who pays their respects and who isn't there but should be. Time to get my head on straight, I've been way too distracted as of late and bad things happen when I stop paying attention. The sound of Emmie's laughter breaks my thoughts and I smile, it's impossible for me not to chuckle when I hear my kid laugh, it's probably a universal thing among parents. I return to the living room and settle into my spot on the couch.

"Who was that?" Gayle asks.

"Doris, she said I forgot to shut down my computer, so she did it for me."

"What would you do without her?" Gayle smiles.

"I don't know."

"By the way, I tried calling you earlier, but you didn't

answer...where were you?"

"Trapped in a meeting. Sorry, by the time I saw that you had called, I was on my way home."

She gives me a raised eyebrow and shakes her head.

"Remember that Emmie and I are going to check out the house tomorrow, our flight leaves at seven tomorrow morning."

"Yeah, I remember. You're taking a car to the airport, right? I've got a heavy workday tomorrow and won't be able to drive you."

"Daddy, are you sure you can't come?" Emmie says in her sweetest voice.

"No, I'm sorry. I'll figure out when I can come soon, ok?"

"Ok.

I turn my attention back to the movie and try to drown out the thought of just another lie.

5

It's Saturday, the day of Jimmy's funeral. Fat rain drops pound on the pavement, steadily and heavily. I remember when I was a kid that my aunt would tell me that if the raindrops were big, heavy, and fast, that the rain wouldn't last very long; let's hope she was right because I forgot to take an umbrella. I enter the church, shake hands with the usual guys, and take my seat somewhere in the middle. I'll give my condolences to his mother and his wife after the graveside service when they finally put him in the ground. Bastard. God rest his soul. I make the sign of the cross even though the conversation I'm having is entirely internal.

I look around the room; churches are fucked. They ask for all kinds of money and donations for the poor, but you think they could sell one of their fucking rugs on the wall to help out the homeless- or maybe not have so much stained glass, or so much gold, or cut back to one chalice instead of the thirteen that are lined up at the front. I sigh and shift in my seat.

>Mike shuffles in beside me, "Did you see the Capelli family?"

>"No, they're here?"

>"Yeah right up there," Mike motions with his forehead.

"The balls on those guys, let me tell y…does Vin know they're here?" I ask.

"Of course, I know they're here. What? You don't think I got eyes and ears all over the fucking place in here? What are you out of your mind?" Vinnie squeezes in between Mike and me, while Charlie and Tommy sit in the pew behind us.

"Relax, Vinnie!" Mike says with a forced smile, "People are starting to stare."

Little old Italian ladies dressed in black, from head to toe, are crinkling their noses and raising their eyebrows at us. One of them kisses her rosary and shoots us a disapproving glance.

I lower my voice and lean into Vinnie, "So what happens now?"

"We bury Jimmy and try not to get killed in the meantime. We'll make our move in the next couple of days."

I lean back in to say something, but Vinnie shushes me, "The service is starting. Shut ya mouth."

The service is long and boring and in Italian. My mind wanders and I think about my aunt's funeral, I was the only person in attendance. There were lilies everywhere, her favorite flower, and for years afterward the smell of them churned my guts. They were a reminder of the crushing realization that the only person who ever gave a damn about me had died. I'm thankful that there are no lilies here, now.

The priest drones on and it's finally over. We wait for Jimmy's wife and his mother to leave the front of the church behind the casket and the rows empty out in order, after them. St. Michaels has a cemetery on the grounds so there will be no loading and unloading the casket into a car to get to the burial site.

We follow the crowd out back and there are a few minutes of organization taking place before the burial, so Vinnie takes the opportunity to light a cigar. The rain had stopped, turns out my aunt was right, but there was no sun, only thick, grey clouds filled the sky.

Jimmy's wife looks good. She places a rose on his casket before it's lowered into the ground.

"Get out of the way!" A woman says as she makes her way to the front. She's wearing a tight black dress and a short black veil with red lipstick, she staggers a bit but looks steady enough on her feet, maybe it's because her five-inch stilettos are sinking into the wet ground. She places a rose on the casket as well, but it's a white one not red.

"The purity of our love will live on, Jimmy. I'll always love you."

Someone gasps and Jimmy's wife says, "Who the fuck are you?"

"I'm Jimmy's TRUE love!"

"Jimmy's true…ARE YOU FUCKING KIDDING ME?" his wife screams.

I glance at Vinnie and the other guys as if to say *can you believe this is happening?* And I know what they're thinking based on the raised eyebrows and smirks I'm getting back from them. Jimmy's wife lunges at what is obviously Jimmy's mistress and grabs a handful of her bouncy blonde hair. The other woman screams and scratches Jimmy's wife across the face. It's officially a shit show. Jimmy's wife's uncle intervenes, and two guys pull the women apart. "What's the first rule of a girl fight?" Mike smirks as he whispers. "Never break it up," I answer. The other woman is removed, by force and is thrown out of the service.

The priest continues and no one can believe what just happened. Not that it was unbelievable that Jimmy had a mistress or anything like that, well maybe that was a little unbelievable because Jimmy was an ugly and miserable fuck, but that she would have the balls to show up at his funeral and take on his wife. Jimmy's wife doesn't shed a single tear from that point on. I'm sure she's cursing him and what she really wants to do is spit on his grave. If his family weren't here, she might have, she's just that type of broad. What's that old saying about a woman scorned? She looks good though, tight black dress, heels with red bottoms, and a black coat. My mind wanders to the time that she showed up at my house in the middle of the night, drunk and wanting to screw.

It was two in the morning and there was a knock at the door. She was there standing on the porch with a half empty bottle of Jack Daniels, almost naked, and totally hammered. I let her in of course and slept with her. When we were finished and she tried to roll over and go to sleep, I kicked her out of bed. I grabbed her by the throat, threw her against the wall, and told her to never show up at my house where my wife and daughter sleep ever again or I'd kill her. I threw her shoes onto the lawn and slammed the door behind her.

We've screwed around a bunch of times since then, never at my house or hers but in hotels, and in back alleys, and public bathrooms. Basically, we did it wherever we could as many times as we could. I don't know what my fascination is with her, maybe it's that she lets me do whatever I want to her and maybe it's because she's not concerned with her level of pleasure-only mine.

I turn my attention back to the service. The priest drones on and Jimmy's mother is wailing; I don't know if it's because she's sad that he's dead or it's because of the circus she just witnessed and all the embarrassment he caused her even after death. Maybe it's both. To say that Jimmy and his mother had a tumultuous relationship would be an understatement. Even with as much shit as she gave him, Jimmy went to visit her every Sunday like clockwork; they had their good days and bad ones, but that's with any family I suppose. I guess it doesn't really matter. The priest finally finishes, and everyone pays their last respects.

This has been the longest day of my life; I just want to get out of here. We see Tony Capelli talking to Jimmy's mother and he embraces her. What the fuck is going on? Something here doesn't add up. Jimmy would be rolling in his grave if he saw this shit; his mother being embraced by a member of a rival family. We each line up to offer our condolences to Jimmy's mother. We give her a kiss on the cheek, some thoughtful words, and then we get the fuck out of there, but not before she loses her shit in Italian on us. I have no idea what she's saying.

Mike translates, "She's saying that it's Vinnie's fault that her son is dead, and she hopes that we all burn in hell."

There's nothing left to say. Vinnie takes a long drag on his cigar as I observe him; the wrinkle in his forehead between his eyebrows is deep, his skin is ashen, and his eyes are dull. He is stressed to the max and with good reason.

"So, what's the next move?" Charlie asks.

"We take one of theirs," Vinnie answers.

"Don't we need some kind of permission for that?" Mike questions.

"It's been cleared," Vinnie says.

And that was all we needed to know.

*

I kick off my shoes and head to the kitchen. I need a beer. Gayle only allows me to buy a case a year, thank fully she doesn't know about my hiding spot in the garage, because of my previous issues with drinking. She also doesn't know about Tuesday night poker games where I drink like a fish because usually, she's at her sister's place overnight. Her sister has some book club thing that she runs each week where a bunch of more than middle-aged women read captivating books that deal mostly with shirtless, hunky men and orgasms- the real riveting literary works of our time. No sooner than I twist the top off and take a drink, does my phone ring; it's my kid.

"Dad?"

"Yeah, sweetheart?" I say as I fumble to hear her on my cell and finish the mouthful.

"When are you coming to see my new place?"

I sigh, "Honey, we talked about this last night and I saw the place, I picked it out remember?"

"I mean, when are you coming to help me get settled?"

"What do you need help with? I paid the bill, isn't that what my part of the agreement was? Your mother is the one that does the decorating and stuff, you guys can arrange the stuff and the movers delivered the furniture already assembled, I'll come when I can ok? I promise, I'm just busy right now, Emmie."

"I know, Dad. I just miss you…"

I raise an eyebrow, "Annnnd…?

She sighs, "And mom is driving me crazy."

"There it is. Do I know my kid, or do I know my kid?" I say. "Sweetheart, that whole missing me thing worked when you were five years old, but I'm on to you now, princess."

"Mom is just being really obnoxious with not letting me express my own style. I have a vision for this place, Dad."

"*You have a vision for the place?*" I repeat and chuckle, "Sweetheart you're not going all Martha Stewart on me, are you? There's only room for one of those in this family and your mother holds the current title. God didn't give me the strength to deal with two of you."

"We're just fighting a lot."

"Already? It's been a few hours and you guys are already at each other's throats?" I shake my head.

"Yeah we just don't see eye to eye on anything. Why is she such a pain?"

"Emmie, one day, my wish is that you will have a daughter who is exactly like you," I say with a smile.

"Hold on a sec, Dad," she says, and a muffled sound fills the line.

"James?" My wife says.

Emmie has obviously reluctantly handed me over.

"Yeah, I'm here."

"Your daughter is impossible," She sighs, "When will you be coming to New York?"

"Gayle, I'm busy, you know that I'll be there as soon as I have a break in my schedule."

"Well things would be a lot smoother if you were here," she mutters.

"I'm not coming all the way to New York to referee things between you two, if I wanted to do that, we could have all just stayed at home."

"James, please! This is important! When are you coming?"

"I'll be there later in the week," I say as I mentally flip through my schedule.

"Good…No! NO! Not over there please, that goes upstairs!" Gayle says to Emmie and I decide it's time to end the phone call before I end up in the middle of their battle.

"Gayle, I'll see you soon ok? Tell Emmie I love her, I gotta go." I disconnect before she can get another word in.

I close my eyes for a second as a smile spreads over my face, I'm so glad I'm not in New York.

*

I open a fourth beer and then a fifth. Before I know it, the case is gone and I'm down a grand on online poker. It's so shitty how online gambling sites rope you in; when you first sign up, they let you win a few bucks and you think you're on a roll. Then you're twelve beers deep and adding more money to your account because you blew it all. I stumble across the room and put the last empty back into the case. I'll have to go get a new case tomorrow so that Gayle doesn't find out that I drank them all.

I could really use some sex right now or a really good blow job. Yeah, a blow job would be amazing. I think about it for a second and then try and talk myself out of what I'm about to do. I grab my keys out of the dish and put on some shoes; It takes a few attempts, but I finally get them on. I trip down the staircase but catch myself before I faceplant into the garden. I unlock the car and buckle my seatbelt because safety first. Where was I going again? Oh yeah, to get laid. Fuck, would it be bad to go to see Jimmy's wife? I mean the guy isn't even cold yet, but…nah fuck it.

I open the window and crank up the volume on the stereo, great song. I turn left onto Avalon and then make a right onto Tapley. I think her house is around here… what was the number again? 215 or 217…damn, I forget. I've only ever been there once before, never to see her, just to drop off Jimmy. I pull into the driveway and the car jerks forward and makes a crunching sound. God dammit, I just hit the bumper of her car, it's a piece of shit so I'm not that worried about it; I'm more worried about mine.

I survey the damage, looks ok from here. It's dark though so I'm not entirely sure that it's ok or not, but I've got one thing on my mind. Climbing the steps of her front porch I take a deep breath and let out a belch. Better to do it here than inside, but it's not like Jimmy's girl is picky or anything, I mean, she did marry Jimmy and he was a disgusting pig.

I push the doorbell and wait, no answer. I push it again and the front porch light goes on; I hear someone clomping down the stairs and the door flies open.

"Can I help you?"

"You're not Jimmy's wife," I blurt and let out a laugh. I can't help it; the dude is built like a linebacker with shoulders I can't see over.

"No, and I'm not Jimmy. You've got the wrong house. Do you know what time it is?"

"No, I'm not wearing a watch," I say.

"Are you drunk?" He asks.

"I've had a few. Listen, thanks for being at the wrong house, I don't know what I would have done if you opened the door to Jimmy's wife's place and were fucking her. I mean, I don't blame you, she's a good piece of ass, but her husband just died, and it wouldn't be very appropriate of both of us to do that."

The guy stares at me for a second and I pray that he doesn't punch my lights out. He seems angry because of the vein throbbing in his forehead and I can see that his fists are clenched.

"I'm calling the cops," he says before he slams the door in my face.

"You don't have to do that!" I shout, "Everything is fine. I'm just here to fuck Jimmy's wife. It's ok because he's dead!"

The door opens again, and the guy is holding a baseball bat. "Listen pal, you better get the fuck outta here right now before I bust open your skull."

I scramble down the stairs and back to the car. I lock the doors and turn the ignition over. The guy is out of his mind and has totally killed my hard on with his manic behavior. Maybe I should just call Jimmy's wife. Shit, I should have done that in the first place. *Where's my phone?* Fuck it. I'm going home. I back out of the driveway and hit a parked car on the street. God dammit, not again! I'm not getting out to check the damage, piss on it.

I make a right turn and then a left when a blinding set of red and blue lights flashing lights fill my rearview mirror. This isn't good. Do I make a run for it or pull over? Not enough time, he's practically on top of me. I pull the car to the side and shut off the ignition. I throw the keys on the floor of the passenger's side and rub my hands over my face. I chew a couple pieces of gum and try my best to look respectable.

"Good evening, sir. Do you know how fast you were going?"

"No."

"You were doing eighty in a fifty."

I stare at him blankly. He leans into the window, "Please show me your license and ownership…have you been drinking tonight, sir?"

I shake my head, "No. I haven't been drinking. Just out for a little fresh air." I reach for the papers in the glove box, but he stops me.

"Sir, I'm going to get you to step out of the car for me."

"Why?"

"Because I believe you're intoxicated."

"Just because you believe something doesn't make it true," I say as I unbuckle my seatbelt and open the door. I steady myself for a second before standing up, everything is spinning.

"I'm going to get you to breathe a real deep breath right into this for me, don't stop blowing until I tell you to."

Talk about irony. I was just on my way to tell Jimmy's wife the same thing. He gives me a pen type thing with a plastic bag on the end of it and I blow.

"Harder…keep blowing…keep blowing…good," the cop says as the instrument beeps.

"Can I go now?"

"No. You're going to turn around and place your hands on the roof of the car. Do you have any drugs on your or anything that could poke or stab me?"

"No," I say as I turn around and follow his instructions. My head is pounding and all I want to do is lay down.

He searches me and comes up empty.

"See? I don't have anything on me."

"That doesn't change the fact that you blew twice the legal limit and are intoxicated while operating a motor vehicle, sir. Put your hands behind your back."

I do as he says, and he slaps a pair of cuffs on me. Shit, this isn't good. I'm put into the back of the police car.

"What about my car? We can't just leave it here."

"I just called for a tow truck. It will be waiting for you in impound, don't worry."

6

Fuck. I'm in a lot of trouble. How could I have been so stupid last night? Now, I'm going to be disciplined by the medical board and maybe even fired. I collect my personal belongings from the desk clerk and Vinnie finishes up the paperwork with the jail administration person. I don't know how I'm going to tell Gayle or what I'm going to do in the meantime. I guess just try and to maintain the status quo. My head is pounding, and I feel like I've fallen out of a twelve-story window. It doesn't pay to be old, stupid, and drunk. The worst part is that I didn't even get laid. Vinnie doesn't say a word as we walk to the car. I'm thankful that he's here to give me a lift home, but I don't want to have the conversation that I know is imminent.

We sit in silence for a few minutes before I speak first.

"Thanks for coming, Vin."

"Charlie is picking up your car. We know a guy at impound. Where were you going when they pulled you over?" Vinnie ignores my gratitude.

"I was headed home," I say as I try and avoid this conversation the best that I can. I'm not in the mood to have it and I don't want to be lectured.

"Where were you coming from?"

And that's the question I was hoping to avoid. I know I'd better tell him the truth; it would be way worse if I didn't and if he found out on his own.

"I was going to see Jimmy's wife."

There's a long bit of silence before Vinnie finally spits, "What the fuck are you thinking, James? I told you to stay away from her, that it was for your own good."

"I was go…" I say and Vinnie cuts me off.

"Shut ya fuckin' face. The guy's funeral was less than twelve hours ago and you're at his house, trying to hook up with his wife when the dirt hasn't even settled? What the fuck is wrong with you?"

I don't say anything for a minute because I can't defend my actions.

"It was a lapse in judgement," I finally say quietly.

"Well, you have a lot of those lately don't you? What are you going to do now?" Vinnie slams the car into park and shuts off the ignition. He raps his fingers on the steering wheel and stares at me.

"What do you mean?" I ask for clarification.

"What do I mean? What the fuck do I mean?" Vinnie screams and pounds the wheel with his fists. "Did you forget about all the money you owe me? Did you think that I forgot?"

"No, Vinnie. I haven't forgotten," I say.

"How do you plan on paying that back? You're probably going to get fired if not suspended from your job…now what?"

"I'll have to figure it out."

"For someone so smart, a fucking doctor, you sure are dumb as fuck. Get out of the car," Vinnie says.

"Vin, I'm sorry," I say as I open the door. "I'll deal with this, and you'll get your money."

He doesn't say a word and peels out of the driveway; this day is getting worse by the minute.

*

I let myself into the house and crawl into bed with all my clothes on. I feel like shit. At least a couple hours of sleep will help a bit. I hear the front door unlock and jump out of bed.

"James?" Gayle yells.

What the hell is she doing here? She shouldn't be home until tomorrow! Shit. I ignore her, rip off my clothes, throw them in the corner, and pull the covers up to my chin. I'll pretend I'm sleeping and that I didn't hear her.

"James!" She yells again as she pushes open the bedroom door.

"Hi Gayle, when did you get in?" I fake yawn and roll over, praying that she buys my performance.

"When did I…are you serious right now? Is there a problem with your phone?"

"No…why?" I stretch.

"Because if you checked any of the seven messages I've left, you'd know that I needed to be picked up from the airport this morning."

I pull the blankets up higher. She rips the duvet off the bed, and I lay there naked as the day I was born.

"I thought you were coming home on Monday…wasn't that the plan?" I sit up.

"Yes, James. That *was* the plan, but not anymore. Again, if you had picked up the phone at least one of the times I called, you'd know that the plan changed."

"So, what's going on?"

She stares at me incredulously, "I don't know what is happening with you, but you had better get it together!" she hisses.

"Let me have a nap and we can talk about this in a couple of hours," I plead. "I'm exhausted, emergency was crowded last night, it was brutal."

"Oh, we're going to talk about this, James. I'm absolutely furious with you right now. You have exactly five minutes to get dressed and meet me in the kitchen."

Gayle leaves the room. What am I going to do? She's this level of pissed about me not answering my phone, wait until she finds out that I have a pending court date for drunk driving and may lose my job…I don't want to think about it right now, so I stop myself from going down the rabbit hole.

I quickly get dressed and head down the staircase; I wish that I had more time to think about what I was going to say and what excuse I was going to use for not answering or returning her calls.

She's sitting at the counter with her hands folded in front of her. I feel like I'm walking into the principal's office and about to get a lecture. As much as Gayle doesn't have a backbone and let's me walk all over her most of the time, she makes me feel like she's the parent and I'm the child. She polices what I eat and what I wear because that's her way of feeling in control, I guess.

"Why are you so angry?" I ask impatiently.

"I'm so angry because you didn't answer any of my phone calls and you didn't have the common courtesy to even *listen* to the messages I left! I needed a ride home from the airport because circumstances have changed, and I need to be at a mandatory meeting tomorrow with the Teacher's Union instead of staying in New York with Emmie for another night!"

"So, what does that mean for me?"

"James! What is going on with you? I'm seriously questioning if you're hearing what I'm saying-I'm back for an emergency meeting with the union, we could be striking, but all you can focus on is yourself and what's going on with your life and schedule, as usual."

I stare at her with nothing to say. I'll just sit and wait until she answers my question.

"That's why I needed to be back today. It would be better if we went to see Emmie next Saturday instead. She's all set up and moved in and I think she just needs time to get her bearings and get settled in. Plus, I'm not ready to turn around and get on another plane in a couple of days. I need a bit of a rest; our daughter takes a lot out of me."

"So, I'm not going to see Emmie at the end of the week? We're going together next Saturday?"

"Yes."

"Ok, that's all I needed to know. I'm going back to bed."

"You're impossible, do you know that?" she says with exasperation.

"James, there's something else we need to talk about."

"What, Gayle?"

"I'm worried about Emmie."

"She's living on her own for the first time and is away from home, it's normal to be worried," I say.

"No, it's not that. I just worry about her and the choices she makes; smoking weed and her choice of friends especially now since she's totally unsupervised. I hate the thought of her being there all by herself with no one to check in on her…"

"Gayle, not the weed thing again, please! It's not a big deal, all kids smoke weed at one point in their lives, that doesn't make them bad kids! Lighten up, Jesus."

"It *is* a big deal! It shows us her lack of judgement! Plus, will she be going to class the next morning after getting high? Will she be in any shape to attend her eight o'clock lectures?

"That's not our problem right now! Why are you anticipating the worst? She's a good kid!"

"I know, I know. I just worry. I wish..." she trails off.

"So, what are you saying?" I'm getting annoyed.

"I'm saying that I wish she was there with someone she knows."

"Gayle! She's not living there permanently, ok? She'll be back every summer and for the holidays, it's not like we're never going to see the kid! Let her have a bit of freedom."

"I want her to at least have a roommate-someone for her to talk to and so that she doesn't have to be in a big empty space all alone."

"Well, she's alone and there's nothing we can do about that. I'm going back to bed. It was a long night at work."

"Fine," she sighs.

I head back upstairs to bed and try to sleep away my hangover.

*

I'm restless now. Gayle's probably right; we should have someone watch over Emmie, but who and how? I dial Vinnie's number. He has contacts in New York and maybe for the time being he can hook me up with someone who can help me keep an eye on my daughter.

"Hello?" the voice on the other end answers.

"Hi, Vin. Listen, I'm really sorry about earlier. I've figured out how I'm going to pay you...I'm going to remortgage the house." I clench my jaw and push the thought of Gayle finding out, out of my mind.

"Good. When will I have my money?"

"Sometime within the next two weeks."

"Good." His demeanor softens and I know as soon as I get him the money, it will all be water under the bridge.

I pause before I ask him for something because I don't know what his reaction will be, "I need help."

"With what?"

"I need someone to watch my kid while she's away at school."

"Which school?"

"NYU."

There's a moment of silence before Vinnie speaks, "Yeah, we can help with that. We've got guys in New York. So, what? You want someone to do surveillance or something like that?"

"Yeah, just keep an eye on her, make sure she isn't getting into trouble."

"Ok. I'll set it up. You're going to have to pay for this kind of service though…you can set that up between you and the guy, let me find his name here, one second…"

I hear him rummaging around and he finally returns to the line, "Ok you're going to contact a guy named Christopher Brunel."

"Christopher Brunel," I repeat and scrawl it down on a piece of paper on the nightstand as Vinnie reads me his phone number.

"Got it?" he asks.

"Yeah. Thanks a million, Vinnie. I appreciate this."

"Let me know if you have any problems. I'll give him a call now to let him know you'll be in contact. Wait for an hour before you call him."

"Thanks, Vin."

*

I hold the paper in my hand staring at the number that Vinnie gave me. Should I do this? Is this me not trusting my kid? What am I going to say to this guy? The clock ticks slowly over the next hour, it's time. I take a deep breath and stop stalling.

"This is Chris," the voice says.

"Vinnie…"

He cuts me off, "Yeah he told me you'd be calling. What do you need?"

"My daughter is at NYU and I need someone to keep an eye on her, make sure she's going to class and staying out of trouble."

"We can do that."

"Thanks," I breathe.

"Let's talk about price."

"Ok. How much is your fee?"

"It's going to be five grand a week."

"Five grand *a week*?" I repeat.

"Yeah. Is that a problem?"

I pause for a beat; the cost of my daughter's safety and my piece of mind would be worth the cost, I remind myself.

"No. No problem."

"Good. This is how it's going to work," he says. "You need to send me her address, a photo of her, and you'll need this account number, 47386902, to wire the money to. The funds need to be deposited each week on Sunday before noon. If you miss a payment, I stop working. That's that. Understood?"

"Yes."

"When should I start?"

"Next Monday."

"Ok. Send me the stuff I asked for so that I can get organized and send the transfer before noon on Sunday, don't forget. I'll call you each week on Saturday to tell you what's been going on and if she's been going to class. She won't see me or even know I'm watching her."

"Good. What's your email address?"

He gives me the email and I scrawl it down beside his phone number.

"I'll send you the photo and address now."

"I'll be in touch," he says and disconnects.

I get off the phone and wonder if I should have asked more questions; I don't know a single thing about this guy and am believing that because he's connected with Vinnie, that he's trustworthy. It's not like I could have interviewed the guy though, what would I have said? *How long have you been doing this? Can I trust you? What if things go wrong, what is my recourse? How do I know that I'm getting my money's worth?* Not much I can do it about it now.

Fuck. This is so unsettling. I should have used the hour beforehand to write down questions, but with these guys, that isn't how this works. It probably would have been taken as an insult now that I think about it; guys like this don't like to be questioned and any little thing can be perceived as disrespect. Then who knows what would have happened; he could have refused to do the job and I'd be back at square one looking for someone to watch over Emmie. And how could I even find someone like that? It's not like those kinds of services are easy to come by. Sure, they've got Private Investigators and stuff like that, but this is something different. Plus, I'd have to hire someone without a recommendation that lives in New York; it's probably better this way.

My laptop is in the office. I flip open the lid and open the photos folder to find a picture of Emmie to send to Christopher. Immediately, I miss my kid. Nostalgia floods over me as I scroll through her photos. I choose one that is most recent and send it to the email. I wish that I could sit here and reminisce, but I've got to go to work. So much for getting some rest.

7

I get to the office and Doris is immediately in my face.

"Dr. Cass, this is Veronica."

I'm not sure what to do, but my face gives me away before I say a word.

"She's going to be your shadow today."

"My shadow?"

"Yes, she's here for part of a co-operative program that we participate in each year with the University. Veronica is studying to be a trauma surgeon."

"Then why isn't she following Dr. Martinez around?" I blurt. "Doris, you know the difference between a trauma surgeon and the head of ER, do you not?"

She smiles tightly, "Veronica, excuse us. We just need a minute, have a seat."

"Doris…" I start.

"What is going on with you?

"I'm sorry. I'm having the worst day and you know I don't like surprises."

She softens, "I know, and this wasn't how this was supposed to work out. Dr. Martinez is off with a horrible case of the flu, the trauma unit is already scrambling, and ER has been buzzing non-stop for the last six hours. Two motorcycle accidents, an overdose, and a car crash are keeping everyone busy."

"Ok, I guess I'll just do what I can do with her."

"And I'll show her as much as I can too, it's only for a few hours today. We can get through it," she pats my arm.

"Yes, we can. I'm sorry, Doris."

"Apology accepted. Oh, and one more thing…"

"What's that?"

"If you ever speak to me the way you did in front of Veronica just now, or in front of anyone for that matter, ever again, I will pack up my things and be out of here. Is that clear?"

"Clear. I'm sorry."

"Good. Now let's get to work. Veronica is waiting."

I go and get the girl and bring her into my office, "Let's start over, I'm Dr. James Cass, head of ER here at the hospital. I understand that you'll be shadowing me for today while Dr. Martinez is off."

"That's correct. I appreciate the opportunity to learn, no matter for how short of a period that is for today. My name is Veronica and I'm a third-year medical student at Stanford. I'm in the top two percent of my class and one day, I hope to be a neurosurgeon."

"Very impressive. Stanford is a great school," I nod.

She glances at my diplomas on the wall and says, "So is North Western."

"Let's get started, we've got a lot to do and we only have a couple of hours to do it in. Doris and I will be splitting your time here today."

"Sounds good, Dr. Cass. I'm ready to learn."

I take her through my day for the next couple of hours and give her a tour of the hospital before dropping her off with Doris.

"All set, Doris. Thanks for being here today, Veronica. Great questions and I think that you'll have much more fun with Dr. Martinez tomorrow. I'm sure I'll see you in the hallways!"

"Thank you for accommodating me at the last minute, Dr. Cass. I had a great day and learned a lot."

I nod and return to my office. Nice kid. If only Emmie showed that much interest in a vocation…she picked liberal arts at NYU…what exactly is liberal arts? It's a program for kids who don't know what they want to do with their lives yet, that's what that is. I gather my paperwork, pull some files, and sit down at my computer. My phone buzzes in my pocket, it's Vinnie.

"Hi Vinnie, what's up?"

"We have reservations for tonight."

"Ok, what time?" I ask. I know that reservation means he's speaking in code and it's when he's planning on the hit.

"Ten o'clock. Stay close to your phone. I may need a ride home."

"Understood." I say and we disconnect.

*

Hours pass and my eyes are burning from all the paperwork I just completed; I need to get away from this screen. I stand up and stretch. My desk phone rings and it's Doris.

"Dr. Cass, we have a bit of a situation," she whispers.

"What do you mean?"

"The police are here, and they want to speak with you."

My heart thuds in my chest, "Did they say about what?"

"No. Should I send them in?"

"No. I'll come out and get them. Be right there."

Fuck. Don't panic. This is exactly what Vinnie said would happen. He said that the cops would be coming around to ask questions. I pour myself a glass of water and head to the admin desk where Doris is standing, waiting.

"Can I help you?" I say to the taller of the two police officers.

"Dr. Cass?"

"Yes, that's right."

"We need to ask you a few questions, do you…"

I interrupt him, "Please, step into my office, we can talk in there, it's less chaotic."

I lead the way as the officers follow behind me. I shut the door and sit down. I offer them a seat, but they decline.

"Dr. Cass, do you know anything about the death of Gianni Romano?"

I shake my head, "Who?"

"Gianni Romano, you may know him as Jimmy."

"Jimmy. Yes."

"So, you know something about his death?" the cop asks.

"No. I know him as Jimmy. That's what I was saying yes to."

The cop smirks, "We're not here to waste your time, Dr. Cass. We just want to ask you a few questions to see if you can help us."

"Ask away."

"Do you know who killed Gianni Romano?" the cop repeats.

"No."

"Where were you on Thursday the 25th at eleven pm?"

"I was here."

"Do you have record of that?"

"In other words, can I prove it? Yeah, I can prove it. You should've spent your time talking to Doris. She's the one that handles my schedule," I smile.

Neither cop is smiling back at me.

"Doris, can you come in here please?" I say through the phone.

"Yes, Dr. Cass."

"And bring your calendar with you."

"Sure. I'll be there in a second."

Doris enters the room with her trusty paper calendar and pen.

"Please show us the schedule for Thursday the 25th," the cop says.

"Of course," Doris complies. She flips to the page and shows them the information.

"I don't understand what you're showing me. Can you please just show me what time Dr. Cass was working that night?"

"Sure, see right here?" Doris points to the page, "Dr. Cass had two car crashes, a bike accident, a gunshot victim, and a kid with a fractured skull who wasn't wearing a helmet while skateboarding."

"I see," the cop says. "And what time was he here?"

"The kid with the fractured skull came in at eleven fifteen. By the time he got to Dr. Cass, it was 12:30 because we were running short staffed and behind schedule. But what else is new?" she quipped.

"Thank you, Ma'am. We have no other questions for you, but we do need a few more minutes alone with Dr. Cass."

"Of course, if there's anything else I can assist with, I'm just outside the door," she says.

"Thanks, Doris," I say.

We sit in silence for a beat.

"Dr. Cass, what's your relationship to Vincent Dicenzo?"

"We're friends, we've been friends for a long time."

"Do you know that he's involved in criminal activity?"

"No."

"He's a dangerous criminal Dr. Cass, but I think you know that."

"I don't know anything other than we're friends and we have been for a long time," I repeat.

"Thank you for your time, Dr. Cass."

"It's been my pleasure," I say as I open the door and show them out.

"Oh, one more thing," the cop says, "You should be careful who you choose as friends. You never know what you could be implicated in. Their mess could be your mess."

"Have a good day, gentleman," I say and shut the door behind them.

I turn off my computer and stuff the papers I need into my briefcase. I'll call Vinnie to let him know about the visit when I get to the car.

*

"Vin, it's James. Can you meet me?"

"Yes, the Deli. Fifteen minutes."

We disconnect and I make my way to the meeting place.

*

I pull into the lot and see Vinnie's Escalade is already there. That means he's already inside waiting.

I push through the doors and Vinnie is smoking a cigar, "What's up, Doc?" Mike, Tommy, and Charlie are there too.

"The police came to visit me today, just like you said they would."

"And what did you tell them," Vinnie asks as he takes a long drag.

"I didn't tell them anything. We weren't involved in Jimmy's death, so there was nothing to say."

"But if we were involved in it would you have said something?"

"No of course not, Vin. You know I hate cops and that I'd never say a word about anything."

"Just making sure."

I pause for a second, "Were we somehow involved with Jimmy's death?"

"Why would you ask that?" Vinnie says.

"Because you just said that if we were involved would I have said something…what does that mean?"

"It means what it means. Of course we didn't have anything to do with Jimmy," he says.

"Ok."

"Now, about our reservations tonight. We need to send a clear message and the only way to do that is to get to the heart of the matter."

"How do we do that?"

"We send them his heart."

I can't believe what I'm hearing, "We what?"

"We rip out his heart and send it to the Capelli family."

"Who's heart, Vin?" Charlie asks.

"Tony's."

"Oh my god, do you think that's a good idea? He's the head of their family, Vin! That would be like them killing you," Mike interjects.

"Shut up, all of you. It's the only way."

We sit there in silence. I don't think we'll be able to change Vinnie's mind, I'm not sure if anything we could say or do at this point would make him bend.

"I know Jimmy was our friend," Charlie says, "But what we're about to do is a bit overkill wouldn't you say? You're going to start a war if you do this, Vin. This is something that's going to be so much bigger than us. Something that could get out of control."

"Don't you think I know the cost? Don't you think I know exactly what's going to happen after this?" Vincent says.

"Why Tony though? What if we picked a lesser guy? Then we

might be able to avoid the worst-case scenario." Mike offers.

"I think it's a better idea, Vin," I say.

"Me too," Tommy says.

Vinnie pauses and thinks about what we've said. I pray that he changes his mind because there's no turning back if he doesn't. If he chooses to go after Tony Capelli, he's basically signing our death warrants.

"So, all of you feel the same way?" Vinnie asks.

"Yes," we nod in unison.

"Let me remind you that this is not a democracy. What I say goes and if I say that we're hitting Tony Capelli, then that's what we're doing…but there may be some merit to what you're saying," he pauses. "We'll leave Tony alone. We'll take his daughter's husband, Joe instead."

"Lemme get this straight, Vin," Mike says, "We're gonna kill Tony's daughter's husband? The daughter that Jimmy was fucking?"

"What did I just say, dipshit?" Vinnie spits.

"Wow. Ok, well I'm just glad we're not hitting Tony," Charlie breathes.

"So, we're in agreement then? We have a reservation with Joe at ten o'clock," Vinnie says.

"Agreed," we say.

"And we're going to rip his heart out?"

Tommy nods, "If that's what you want to do, then that's what we'll do, Vin."

"Good, now let's get the fuck out of here. I'm starving. Oh, and one more thing, James…you're not invited to tonight's festivities; it's members only."

"I understand," I say and try to hide the relief in my tone.

"Plus, you've got something else you need to do," Vincent says.

"I know. I'll have it to you within the next few days," I say.

We leave the deli and I know that I have to work quickly. I'm running out of time.

8

I swing by the house to change my clothes. Gayle's car is gone, and I breathe a sigh of relief; she's probably at yoga or some hot stone massage thing that she goes to once a week. I'm glad she's not here because she'd want to know why I'm not at work and whatever answer I gave would turn into an argument.

I need to look my best if I'm going to ask the bank for a loan. That may be an old, outdated way of thinking, but a lot of people, most people in my opinion, dress much too casually nowadays; I believe that everyone should dress the way that they want to be addressed. I've tried to drill that belief into Emmie's head, but I'm not sure it stuck based on some of her outfits I've witnessed. Hopefully, she'll grow out of the ripped jeans and crop top stage sooner than later. My thoughts turn from my today's fashion to the matter at hand; I need to find out what my financial options are. I'd much rather owe the bank than Vinnie because the bank won't murder me if I can't pay…they'll just take everything I own, but at least I'll still have my life. I put on my best suit and tie even though it feels like it's a thousand degrees outside, and head back out the door.

*

The bank parking lot is empty which is a good sign, I hope. That means that they aren't super busy and can probably see me. I didn't bother to book an appointment, maybe I should have. I'll take my chances and see if I can get in. Worst case scenario, I'll make an appointment for another day, but I really don't want to do that. I just want to get this whole owing Vinnie money thing, over with. It weighs on my mind every single day and is causing me a ton of stress.

The fingerprints on the glass door are disgusting. Don't they have people around to wipe off the glass?

I approach the desk and a young man greets me, "Hello. What can I help you with today?"

I was right about people dressing much to casually, the guy that works here is case in point with his dark wash jeans and green short-sleeved polo shirt. I guess I'm just behind the times, but since when should people that work in a bank be allowed to dress so casually? They deal with hundreds of thousands if not millions of dollars' worth of people's money that dressing well is merely a form of respect. A way for them to say to every person that walks in here, *Trust us, you're in good hands.*

"I'm here to talk about refinancing my home or getting a loan."

"Sure. I trust you've made an appointment with one of our advisors?"

"Yes," I lie.

"Great. What's your last name?"

"Cass."

"And first name?"

"James."

He pauses and I know that he can't find my non-existent appointment in the system.

"That's odd. We don't have you scheduled. Are you sure it was this branch?"

"Yes. It was for today."

"Do you remember the name of the advisor you requested?" He asks without looking up.

I glance down the hall and read the first name plate that I can see clearly, "It was Jamieson, I don't remember the first name, I'm sorry."

"Ah, that's ok. There must have been a mix up or a glitch in the system. Let me check a couple of things."

"No problem."

"Hmm, I still can't find you in the calendar, but hang tight and I'll see if Doug can see you yet, he may just be wrapping things up because you're fifteen minutes early. Can I get you a coffee?"

"No, I'm fine. Do I just wait over here?" I ask, motioning to a group of chairs.

"Yeah, that's perfect. I'll call you when he's ready."

I sit down in the hideous green, leather chairs that are probably a breeding ground for germs. I'm careful not to touch anything. I wait for about fifteen minutes before the guy who I assume is Doug, comes out to greet me. He extends his hand for me to shake and introduces himself. He's another one that's wearing jeans! *What is going on in the world?*

"Doug Jamieson at your service. Sorry about the mix up with the calendar; step into my office and let's chat."

He leads me into the room and offers me a seat. He sits across from me on the other side of the desk and logs into his computer.

"So, what are we here to talk about?"

"I need money."

He chuckles, "How much money to be exact?"

"One hundred and fifty thousand dollars."

"Ok, let's see what we can do." He types on his keyboard and asks me the relevant information that he needs to pull up my financials.

"What do you need the money for?"

"I'm going to renovate my home office and get a new roof."

"Sounds good."

"Can we do a home equity loan?" I ask.

"Um, I'm afraid not. According to what I'm looking at your debt ratio is too high for us to extend that amount of money to you by any means of credit."

"What do you mean?"

"I mean between the credit cards, lines of credit, the refinancing of your home last spring, and the equity you've already taken out, we can't extend you any type of credit. I'm sorry."

"What about a lesser amount?"

"Let me punch in some numbers and see what the program says."

"The highest amount that I'd qualify at this point, I'll take."

"Hmm…Unfortunately, there's just no wiggle room," he says.

"I *really* need this money," I say as my heart thuds against my ribcage. What the fuck am I going to do if I can't secure the cash I need to pay my debt to Vinnie? "Is there anything you can do? *Anything*? I make a lot of money; I don't understand what the problem is."

"At this point in time I'm sorry, there's no way that I can help. Even if you paid off all the credit cards, there still wouldn't be room for the amount that you're asking for. It's not about how much money you make, it's about the risk to us as a lender and your debt ratio."

Fuck. Now what?

"So, there's nothing that can be done? What about another bank?

"I'm sorry, I can't speak for another bank, and unfortunately, I think the answer would be the same. You have too high of a debt ratio."

"Thank you for your time," I say as I stand up.

"I wish I could have helped you. Have a good day."

*

I rest my head on the steering wheel. I need cash and I need it fast. I have no money, no plan, and no way out of this mess. My phone rings; it's an unknown number. I hesitate to answer it, but my gut tells me I should. I pick up on the fourth ring.

"Hello?"

"James, it's Phil. I need you back at the hospital. It's important."

Fuck. Phil is my boss and the main guy in charge of everything that goes on in my department. The order of rank goes Frank, Phil, and then me. Frank is the big boss; thank god he's not calling me because then I'd really be shitting bricks.

"Why? What's going on?"

"James, it's better if you come in. We need to talk. When can you meet me?"

"Give me half an hour."

"See you soon."

*

The whole way to the hospital I think about how much they know. Do they know about my pending court date for drunk driving? They must, plus if they don't know by now, they will, it's only a matter of time. Is it something else? I rack my brain trying to think of what else it could be, and I fight to steady my hands on the wheel.

*

Doris' face says it all as I walk by her desk.

"What's going on?" I whisper.

"I was hoping you'd tell me!" she answers.

I walk into my office and Phil is sitting with his back to me. He stands when I enter the room.

"Thanks for being here," he says.

"Is everything ok?" I ask while I hang up my jacket.

"No, James, everything is not ok. Take a seat."

I do as he says, and I place my hands on my knees to stop them from shaking under the desk.

"I understand you have a pending court date for a drinking and driving incident, it that correct?"

"Yes," I say without hesitation.

Phil pauses and shifts his weight in the chair, "James. This is the second incident of alcohol-based problems you've been involved in."

"I know, and I'm sorry."

"What is going on with you?"

I pause for a moment. How can I tell him anything? And where would I start? That I'm in deep with some bad people and that I owe them a hundred and fifty grand because of a gambling debt? That my kid is moving away to New York because she wants to get as far away from me and Gayle as possible? That I cheat on my wife and that I don't really love her, but she stays married to me because she loves me more that I could ever love her back? Fuck no! Of course I can't tell him my problems; he'd think I was crazy and who knows if he'd even believe me.

"I think you need help, man," he says, breaking the silence. "I'm saying that to you as your friend and colleague, not just as your boss. This is bad. We made the other incident go away, but this one is too big. Now the police are involved, and we can't contain it."

"I understand. Thanks for saving my job the last time, Phil. I appreciate everything you've done, I really mean that."

"You know I care about you. James this is bad! Really, really bad!" Phil rubs his face with his hands.

I know you do. Thank you for caring. What happens now?"

Phil takes a deep breath and concern spreads over his face, "Effective immediately, you are suspended with pay, pending the outcome of your court case...I'm sorry James. It kills me to do this, but you've given me no other choice; my hands are tied and it's a damn shame because you're a hell of a good doctor, one of the best in my opinion and the best head of ER we've ever had. We go back a long time."

"I'm sorry, Phil. I know that you've already gotten me out of this situation bef..."

He interrupts me mid-sentence, "James this is so much *bigger* than hiding a bottle of Grey Goose in your desk and drinking on the job. I blame myself for this because if I hadn't let that slide and brushed it under the rug, you probably would have got the help you so desperately need. I saved your ass once; I can't do it again. I'm sorry. You'll have an official meeting with the medical review board once they get wind of your court date. I haven't let the cat out of the bag yet, and in suspending you now, I'm protecting my own ass. I don't want this coming back to me and them saying that I knew and didn't do anything about it."

"I understand," I say weakly.

"Good. James, please get some help. I'll be praying for you."

He stands up and leaves my office. I pack up the things that I need and lock the door behind me for the last time. Doris is not at her desk; part of me is thankful that she isn't because I don't know how I would tell her that I've been suspended. I'm embarrassed and ashamed and Phil's right, this isn't the first time. I guess I thought I was untouchable. And I was for a while, but I suppose everyone's luck runs out at one point or another. I need to go home.

*

As I pull in the driveway my phone rings; it's Vinnie.

"Hi, what's up?" I breathe.

"Just wanted to tell you that the reservation was cancelled last night, so our dinner plans have been postponed for a week."

"What happened?"

"Our guest came down with a nasty case of the flu. We were supposed to meet him at work, but he never showed. He's laid up in bed at his house and we can't have dinner there."

"Understood. So, when is the rescheduled date?" I ask.

"One week from today. I'll let you know if anything changes," he says.

"Ok."

"James, what about my money. How is your plan for repayment working out? When can I expect it?"

"Vin, I've run into a problem. Turns out I'm totally maxed. The bank won't touch me with a ten-foot pole and I'm out of options for refinancing or getting a loan. And today, I've been suspended from work. I'm probably going to get fired. It's only a matter of time."

There is silence on the other line as I wait for his reaction. He doesn't say anything, so I continue.

"Vin is there any way that we can work out another way for me to repay you?"

"There may be."

"Tell me what it is, Vin and I'll do it. I'll do anything."

"Anything?" he asks.

"*Anything*," I repeat. "Please, just work with me here."

"Well, there's only one thing I can think of. You're actually the perfect man for the job."

"Ok," I coax him.

"Our steak needs to be cooked and we want to do it in the most efficient way possible. You're the only guy I know that will be able to keep the cow alive while inflicting as much pain as possible before it dies."

Goosebumps prick my skin.

"If I butcher the cow, my debt will be wiped clean?"

"Yes. Do we have an agreement?"

"I have no other choice," I say.

"Good. I'll be in touch," Vinnie says, and he hangs up.

I open the car door; my legs feel like rubber as I climb the porch steps.

9

"Gayle? Hello?" I shout as I throw my keys into the bowl on the hallway side table, no answer.

I'm still on edge from the phone call with Vinnie just now, but I can't think about it because I'll go insane. I turn my thoughts to my immediate environment. I guess I'm home alone again. It's weird because I don't mind coming home to an empty house; there's something to be said about being alone and being able to decompress for a bit as soon as you walk in the door. No, how was your day? Or what should we have for dinner? And no bitching about not taking the garbage out or whining how the lawn needs mowing. I've had a stressful enough day so the last thing I need is a lecture.

I didn't realize how hungry I am until now. I open the fridge to see what we have; I grab a handful of grapes but put them back when I see some turkey slices hidden behind a block of cheese. I'll make myself a sandwich and take the chance of ruining my dinner because I'm starving. Gayle is in the habit of eating things that are pretty healthy, and I'd be lying if I said I didn't miss chicken wings and pizza. She constantly reminds me that I need to make good choices because I shouldn't preach one thing to our daughter and then do another. She's not telling me anything I don't already know and it's not like to odd greasy, fatty meal is going to be the end of me. Sometimes I get so sick of her rules and I often feel like the child in this marriage. Where is she anyway? She's usually home by now and there's nothing marked on the kitchen calendar and no note left on the counter where they're usually found. I turn on the tv to see four grown women fighting in bikinis while I butter the whole grain bread and rummage through the fridge for the mustard. Reality television keeps getting better, there may be no story line, but partial nudity is always ok with me.

I glance at the clock and see that it's 4:30; I imagine that Gayle will be bursting through the door at any minute or that she'll return home later and yell at me for not knowing where she was because she's told me "*a hundred times*". Maybe I'll just let sleeping dogs lie for a while. I flip to the Sports Network and check the scores from the game the night before. God dammit, Houston again! Unbelievable! I bet on that game and it cost me a grand…why does Chicago always let me down? I lob the remote onto the couch and return to my sandwich. I crack open a sparkling water which tastes like static on a television, and grimace; how anyone drinks this stuff is beyond me.

*

I must have dozed off. I jerk away from a dream about snakes and check my watch, I've been asleep for two hours. I should shower and go to bed for a bit. Gayle still isn't home…Should I call Emmie to see where she might be? But then again, how would she know where her mother is? She doesn't live here anymore and the only thing she would be able to tell me is that Gayle isn't with her. I glance out the window; It looks like it's going to rain, I should bring the pool cushions in. I slide open the patio doors and make my way to the pool. *What is that?* I squint to get a better view.

The blood drains from my head and my heart pounds like a drum. I dive into the deep end with all my clothes on as panic rips through my chest and I drag her onto the deck. I perform CPR on the lifeless, cold body of my wife. I pump her chest and breathe into her as I repeat the words of a famous song that carries the beat to the CPR course on how to save a life. I check her pulse, still nothing. Her fingers and lips are blue, and her body is limp. Thoughts scatter through my brain and I push them away. My only thought is that I need to save my wife. I try again and again, but it's no use. I can't get her heart to start and she won't breathe. I try for an hour. And then another. And then I hold her in my arms and sob. *What happened?* I need to call 911. I know that she's dead, but I still need to call. The wind is picking up and the clouds are moving in. I need to call 911. I already said that. I can't leave her by herself out here, it seems cruel and indignant. I'm shaking, I have to call. How did this happen? Why wasn't I home? What if I could have stopped this? What if something I could have done would have prevented this?

I gently lay my wife down on the cold concrete and rush into the house to grab my cell phone. My hands are shaking as I dial 911 on my keypad. "My wife is dead, I found her dead in the pool," is all I can manage to blurt out. The dispatcher is asking me questions, I have no answers. My mind is blank, and I can only picture Gayle alive. I feel like I'm dreaming. I start sobbing again and return outside to my wife. Is this really happening?

The sky opens up and the rain starts to pour. I can't let her stay like this, but I shouldn't move her anymore before the paramedics get here, the police will be coming too. I sit beside her in the rain and let it wash over us. Thoughts pour out of my brain and spill out of my mouth just like the rain falls from the sky.

"I'm sorry, please forgive me, I was a terrible husband, I never meant to hurt you," is what I keep repeating out loud.

I just want her back. I want things back to the way they used to be, problems and all, all I want is my wife to be alive. Time drips slowly as if it's moving in reverse. Am I dreaming? Am I still on the couch watching the Sports Network, eating my sandwich? Please let this be a nightmare. I'm startled by a voice.

"Sir? Can you tell me what happened?"

"My wife is dead," I say.

"I'm sorry for your loss. Can you tell me what happened?" He repeats. The other medic is working on Gayle.

"I gave her CPR, but it was too late, she's dead," I say numbly.

"What happened before that?"

"She was in the pool."

"Did you see her swimming?"

"No?"

"How long do you think she's been out here?"

"I don't know."

I watch the paramedic pump her chest and breathe into her lifeless body. He keeps trying to no avail and can't bring Gayle back to life.

"Sir, I'm sorry, your wife is deceased. We have to wait for the coroner to give us the time of death," the cop says to me.

There are two of them one speaks to me and the other doesn't. He tries to make small talk with me, but I'm not in the mood to talk; perhaps it's because he doesn't know what to say or that the good cop bad cop act comes later. I'm sure this guy is the good one because he has to be. But, then again, is there such a thing as a good cop?

"He's on his way, he's about 45 minutes from here, but will come as soon as he can."

Again, I remain silent. What am I supposed to say? Gayle is dead. I can't believe it. A thousand thoughts race through my mind and then the guilt sets in. How can she be dead? She didn't deserve to die. I should be the one that's dead. She deserved a better husband. I shouldn't have cheated on her and lied to her and I should have been more patient. A male voice breaks my concentration.

"Mr. Cass, I'm Coroner Clifton. I'm sorry about your loss. I need to ask you a few things."

"Ok." I say and rub my hands across my face as if to reset myself.

"What is your relationship to the deceased?"

"She's my wife…was…is," I mutter and choke back the tears.

"Where did you find her?"

"Outside in the pool."

"At approximately what time was that?"

"4:30 I think."

The coroner talks with the cops while I sit there completely numb. I feel exhausted all of the sudden. My phone rings and I stare at the screen, it's work.

"You can go ahead and answer that if you need to, we're just about wrapped up here," the coroner says.

I answer it on the next ring.

"Hello?"

"Dr. Cass, it's Doris. What in the world is going on, I come into work and they told me that you've been put on leave! What is happening? No one will tell me anything."

"Gayle is dead," I blurt.

"Pardon?"

"She's dead. I found her in the pool"

"Oh my god, Dr. Cass! I'm so sorry! What happened? Is there anything that I can do?"

I don't' know which question to answer first so I don't answer any of them.

"Oh my god. I'm so sorry," she repeats. Please let me know if there's anything that I can do to help. Again, I'm so sorry."

"Thank you, Doris."

I disconnect and let out a breath. She thinks I'm on leave because Gayle is dead, she has no clue about the drinking and driving incident.

The coroner speaks, "Dr. Cass, the time of death is approximately 2:30 this afternoon and the cause of death will be revealed after an autopsy."

"Thank you," I say. "Any ideas on what could have been the cause?"

"I can't say for sure until the autopsy of course, but in my opinion, I would say it was a heart attack or maybe an aneurysm. She was deceased before she hit the water."

I feel sick to my stomach.

"I don't want an autopsy."

"That's certainly your choice."

I feel off balance and hot.

"Dr. Cass, are you alright?"

"No. I need to sit down," I slump into a deck chair and clench my eyes shut. My palms are sweating, and my heart is racing. I feel like I'm going to pass out. I steady myself and finally open my eyes after the vision of Gayle, lifeless in the pool, takes over my brain.

"Is there a funeral home that you prefer?"

"Yes, Smith's."

"Ok, I'll call them, and the home will assist with the transportation of your wife. You can make arrangements with them for anything further. I'll be on my way."

"Thank you," I whisper.

He leaves and the only thing now left to do is wait. The good cop calls the funeral home and within an hour the workers are in my driveway.

"We'll bring Mrs. Cass to the parlor and keep her comfortable until you're ready," the blonde, younger one says.

What a weird thing to say, *keep her comfortable*? How much more comfortable can she get? She's dead. I guess it's a tricky business to be in and sometimes the words don't sound right. I don't know.

"Dr. Cass?" He says and interrupts my train of thought.

"Thank you. Do I need to make an appointment for the funeral service? How does this work?"

"Here's my card. You can call tomorrow morning and we can book an appointment for that afternoon. Please bring the clothing that you'd like Mrs. Cass to be dressed in. You'll get a chance to review things right down to the last detail and we're happy to guide you through the process."

"Ok." I take the card from him. My pockets are soaking wet, so I place it on the table beside the deck chair, under Gayle's half-empty teacup so that it won't blow away.

"If there's anything you need, please don't hesitate to call."

"Thank you."

The cop speaks next, "Dr. Cass, we're finished here. Again, we're sorry for your loss. Take care."

"Thank you," I repeat.

My wife is placed into the back of a hearse and carted away. The tears come hard and fast when I think about how I'm going to tell Emmie.

10

"Emmie, we need to talk. Please call me back, it's an emergency."

I put my phone on the table; at this point, there's nothing that I can do except wait. I suppose l can call the funeral home in the meantime to set up an appointment. What should she wear? What type of service? What about an urn? The one thing that I know for sure is that Gayle wanted to be cremated; other than that, I have no clue about any of her wishes. Part of me feels guilty for that, like I didn't really know her in some ways. I don't know what her favorite flowers are, or what song should play during the service because we never really talked about it. She had brought it up a few times over the years and each time I told her she was being morbid and brushed her off; there were a lot of times when I brushed her off.

One particular incident still stands out in my mind and I think about it often. I was golfing on a trip with the guys and Gayle called. I was going to ignore her call like I usually did, but that time I answered. She asked me how the trip was going and asked why I let her know everything was ok when we got there. I said to her, "I don't feel like talking to you, actually, I don't want to have anything to do with you." I remember the sound of silence on the other end and what she said to me next. She said, "Wow. Ok. We'll you don't have to tell me twice. No problem, I get it." And she hung up on me. I didn't hear a word from her the rest of the week. Things massively changed between us after that, it's like I could pinpoint it down to that exact day. She never looked at me the same after that and I knew that it was just another thing that pushed her away. It's funny because I spent our whole marriage pushing her away and all she did was love me. All she did was wait for me at home and stay faithful to me throughout the years even when I was texting other women and talking to them in secret and deleting my conversations with them on my phone so she wouldn't find out….but she knew about all of that, and she was still a good wife. I didn't deserve her. She had her faults of course, but she loved me with all of her heart. That's more than I can say about what I felt for her.

The worst part is that I never really wanted to marry her. I waited for eight years to propose to her and the only reason why I did, was because she said if I didn't, that she was going to marry someone else. The truth is, I didn't care about marriage and I wasn't sure she was the right one for me. On our wedding day, I could barely look at her. All of our wedding photos together are with me looking off in the distance, it's almost as if I was *looking for something better*, she'd say when she was upset. The wedding photos ended up being taken down and put in a box in the basement because she couldn't look at them anymore…that was the day after I told her I didn't want anything to do with her.

I really was a miserable fuck during the entire time we were married. Sure, we had our good times, but I never let myself be happy. And if I wasn't happy, I was sure as hell going to make sure that Gayle wasn't either. Any time that she'd get a little too enthusiastic or excited about something, I'd push her down and rain on her parade. I called her pretty much every name in the book including the c-word and I once told her that I wanted to *bash her skull in until she died*. I always thought she brought out the worst in me, but now I know that I brought out the worst in myself.

Buzzing interrupts my thoughts, "Hi Emm."

"What's wrong? Sorry it took me so long to call you back, I was getting a coffee with a new friend, her name is Katie. We met on campus at the bookstore while both looking for the same book and then we realized they only had one copy in stock and the rest were back ordered and..."

"Where are you, Emm?"

"I'm at home now, Dad. What's going on?"

"Mom passed away today."

There's silence on the other end followed by quiet sobbing.

"Sweetheart, I'm so sorry," my voice breaks, and tears rush down my face. The hardest part about being a parent is not being able to hold your kid while they cry, no matter how old they get. Her sobs rip through me.

"How?"

"Heart attack or aneurysm," I say. "She didn't suffer."

There's more quiet sobbing on both of our parts before Emmie finally speaks again.

"I'm sorry I had a fight with her. I'm sorry that I was so short with her and that I was so impatient."

I stop her from continuing, "Emm, don't do this to yourself. Please. You didn't do anything wrong and shouldn't have any regrets. No regrets, ok? Sweetheart, kids fight with their parents all the time, that's a normal part of life."

"I know, Dad. I just feel so shitty."

"I understand completely...so do I."

"Now what happens?" she sniffles.

"Now, I plan the funeral."

"Dad, I don't think…"

"Emmie, I know. It's ok. I can handle this alone, ok? What I could use your help with though is the type of flowers we should have and what she should wear."

"Isn't she being cremated?"

"Yes, but we need to figure out what she's going to wear for that?"

"Oh…so the whole thing gets burned together?"

"Yes."

"Oh."

Silence hangs in the air and neither one of us knows what to say next.

"When is the funeral?"

"Later this week. I'm going to the funeral home today to decide everything. You need to come home, Emm. Use the credit card to book your flight, ok? I don't care how much it is, just get here, please."

"Ok. I'll email my professors and let them know what's going on."

"Good. Keep me posted on your flight, ok? I'll come and pick you up."

"I'll text you later once it's booked."

"We'll get through this, Emm. I love you."

"I love you too, Dad."

I sit for a minute and think about what needs to happen next. I call the funeral home and get dressed to go.

*

I enter the parking lot of Smith's Funeral Home and sit there for a few moments before going inside; all of this feels surreal. I wish Emmie were here or maybe I just wish that I didn't have to do this alone. I get out of the car and push through the front doors of the building.

"Good afternoon, Dr. Cass, my name is Greg Leslie and I'm the manager here," he holds out his hand for me to shake so I shake it. He's dressed in a grey suit with a white shirt and checkered tie. I feel underdressed compared to him.

"Good afternoon."

"We're deeply sorry for your loss."

"Thank you."

"I understand that you're here to make Mrs. Cass' final resting arrangements."

"Yes."

"Please, let me tell you a bit about the amenities here so that you can make an informed decision."

For the next hour I'm taken on a tour of the place and shown all the options for Gayle's service, cremation, and flowers. It's a relatively smooth process and for that, I'm grateful.

"Thank you for coming today, Dr. Cass. I know this is difficult, but please know that we're here for you. If we can be of any further assistance, please let us know and we are happy to help."

"Thank you. I think everything is covered. I appreciate your guidance."

"It's our pleasure. See you in a few days," he says.

We shake hands once more and I'm glad that it's finally over. I think I chose well, but I can't be sure; I hope Gayle would have liked what I'd chosen for her. I guess I'll never know.

My phone dings as I get back into the car; it's Emmie texting me that her flight comes in tomorrow afternoon at two. I text her back:

Everything is picked out for Mom. I hope that you like what I chose.

I'm sure it's perfect. See you tomorrow, Dad. I love you.

I love you too, Emm. See you tomorrow.

*

There's a tapping sound coming from somewhere. *What the hell?* I rub the sleep out of my eyes and see a red cardinal bashing its beak against the bay window. Maybe it's staring at its reflection or something or maybe it thinks there's another bird and is fighting it. I stretch and check the time on the alarm clock; it reads 9:07 am. I have a couple of hours before I need to pick up Emmie from the airport. I don't really know what to do with myself until then; there's no work to do for the hospital since I've been suspended, and I don't want to swim in the pool. I'm not sure I can ever go back in the pool since the memory of Gayle floating dead in it is burned into my brain. There are some things that just can't be unseen. I'm mulling around the idea of selling the house, but then I think of my kid. She grew up here, there are marks on the wall in her bedroom that measured her height each year on her birthday as a child, and there are memories with Gayle here. If I sell the house, it would be like I'm extinguishing those memories; I don't want to forget anything…except for all the times I was cruel to her and all the times that I betrayed her. My phone rings and the caller identification displays *unknown number.*

"Hello?"

"Hi. Is this James?"

"Yes, who is this?"

"It's Chris. I've got an update on your daughter."

"What?"

"I followed her to the bar last night, she hung out with a couple of guys and one other girl."

"Ok? Is there anything that I should be concerned about?"

"Well, I don't know at this point. She made it home at around two this morning and now she's headed toward the airport. I just want to remind you that I don't do anything internationally, I'm not getting on a plane to follow her…not for free, anyways."

"So what you're telling me is that my daughter went out for a couple of drinks last night, made it home safely, and now is headed for the airport to come and see me and attend her mother's funeral?

"I don't know why she's going to the airport. Like I sai…"

I cut him off, "This is what I'm paying you five grand a week for? *This* is the type of intel that I can expect? Are you fucking kidding me? You better get your shit together and start telling me relevant information. I want detailed logs of where she goes and who she's with, if she's going to class, if she's doing drugs, and all the shit that parents need to know about when they can't keep an eye on their kid. That's why I hired you, dipshit." If I could reach through the phone and strangle him I would.

"You never said that."

"What?"

"Said what?"

"That you wanted detailed logs and all of that shit. You should have been clear from the very beginning."

"What did you think I wanted? I want you to keep an eye on my daughter!"

"I am. I told you she went out and that she was going to the airport."

I can't take anymore.

"You'd better start doing a better job or I swear to god, I'll come to New York and deal with you myself, face to face. And you can forget about being paid for your services."

"You paid me for this week. That's the price of the information that I sent you."

"I'm not paying you next week if this is what I can expect."

"You stop paying, I stop reporting. Plain and simple."

I take a deep breath before I lose my mind on him.

"Just get me the information I asked for and we won't have any problems. I'll talk to you in a week," I say and hang up on him.

I knew this was a bad idea; I knew it was bad from the second I decided to spy on my daughter.

*

"It's good to see you, sweetheart."

"You too, Dad," Emmie says as we embrace. She cries into my shoulder and I hold her as her entire body shakes. I hug her a little tighter.

"It's ok, it's ok. Everything is ok, Emm. We'll get through this, together."

I grab her suitcase and throw it in the trunk as she gets into the car.

"Dad?"

"Yes?"

"Is everything good with you? I mean, other than mom's death…"

"Why would you ask me that, Emm? What do you want to know?"

"I just want to make sure I'm not going to lose both of you."

Her words plunge into my chest like a knife.

"I promise that I'm ok. Emm. You're never going to lose me; I'm always going to be here."

She squeezes my hand and I squeeze back. We talk about a lot of things on the way back to the house; I ask her how things are in New York, how her classes have been, and if she's made friends.

"Things have been going well…I don't want you to freak out, Dad," she says and my heart thuds in my chest in anticipation of her next words.

"I won't freak out…" I say, unsure if I'm able to keep that promise.

"Something weird is going on."

I stay silent for a moment.

"What do you mean?"

"I don't know how to explain it."

"Try your best."

"Ok. At the risk of sounding insane, here goes; I feel like I'm being watched."

"You're being followed or something?" I ask.

I better have a talk with Chris and tell him to keep his distance. He's getting too close and she's noticing him. Fuck, he's got to be the worst private investigator ever. I don't know if I should even give him that title since he's got no qualifications and just came as Vinnie's recommendation.

"No. I don't think so. I just feel like sometimes someone is watching me, but when I turn around to check, everything looks normal."

"Sweetie, just stay alert, ok? And if you notice anything weird, let campus security know. If you're out somewhere like a pub or library or whatever, let the security guards know that you're feeling unsafe. Don't go anywhere alone. It's sad that we have to talk about this, but the truth is, it's reality. And if you can, stay in a group or at least with one other friend."

"Ok, I'll do that. It's probably just my imagination. I'm in a new place and it's just taking some getting used to."

"And remember that you can always call me, and I'll be there as quickly as I can."

"Thanks, Dad."

"There's something that maybe we should talk about, I just want to put it out there as an option and you don't have to give me an answer right away."

"Ok," she says with a raised eyebrow.

"You can always move home. California has some great liberal arts schools and…"

She cuts me off, "Dad, can we please not talk about this right now? I know that you want me to move home with mom gone and everything, but…"

"Ok, you're right, I'm sorry. I shouldn't have said anything, I just wanted to let you know that you're always welcome to come home. The door is always open. This is your home, Emm."

"I know, Dad. This is a conversation for another day."

"I understand, you let me know when you're ready to talk and I'll listen."

"Are you hungry?" she asks.

"I could eat," I say.

"Good, because I'm starving!"

We pull into her favorite fast food restaurant and order the same thing that she's always ordered since she was a kid. It feels good to have her here and it feels good to have some normalcy back in my life even if just for a moment.

11

It is the morning of Gayle's funeral and I'm feeling so much guilt. Last night I had a nightmare; she came to me in my sleep and read me a detailed list of the things that I had done to her. She stood in front of me and I was shackled to a chair in the middle of a courtroom. As she read the list of my transgressions, I cried; I begged her to forgive me, but she wouldn't. She then morphed into all the women that I had cheated on her with and asked my why she wasn't enough. She told me she was taking Emmie and that I would never see either of them again; she said that my choices brought us to this point and that she could never forgive me for destroying our family.

I splash cold water over my face and try to cleanse the nightmare from my memory. I throw on a shirt and pair of shorts before I check on Emmie. She's sound asleep in her bed and looks like an angel. It's so odd how people look so much younger when they're asleep; she looks like a little girl still, and maybe that's just because I'm her father and I'll always see her that way. Or maybe it's because she's in such a peaceful state with nothing to worry about, no thoughts or constant chatter from her mind about anything.

There are so many things that need to be done for Gayle and I don't know if I have the strength to do them. I need to donate her clothing, give Emmie the most special pieces of her jewelry, put the rest in a safety deposit box until Emmie is older, call the bank, close her accounts, change the household bills into my name, and figure out whether I'm keeping her car or selling it. I'm so overwhelmed and have no idea where to start, but these things can be done later. I can take my time doing them and not everything needs to be rushed.

"Good morning," Emmie says as she saunters into the kitchen still half asleep.

"Good morning, how was your sleep?" I ask as I give her a kiss on the forehead and pass her a glass of milk.

"I feel like I've been asleep for days," she says as she takes a sip.

I smile, "I know what that feels like. How about some bacon and eggs?"

"Can we have waffles and bacon instead?"

"Sure," I say as I rummage around for the waffle iron.

We eat our breakfast in almost silence. Neither one of us knows what to say and I'm afraid that if I speak first, I'll start crying.

"It feels like mom is about to walk through the door, or come down the stairs at any second," Emmie says.

I swallow hard, "I was thinking the same thing. It's going to be weird for a while, I'm sure."

"Yeah," Emmie says solemnly.

I clear the breakfast plates and cups and put them in the dishwasher.

"What time do we have to be ready?"

"We've got an hour and a half until we need to be at the funeral home."

"Ok, I'll start getting ready. I forgot to ask you, what did you end up choosing for mom to wear?"

"Her black Chanel skirt and jacket."

Emmie smiles slightly, "She would have liked that."

"Go get ready, sweetheart," I say as I turn away from her so that she won't see the tears welling in my eyes.

*

"I thought there would be people here," Emmie whispers to me as we enter the funeral home chapel.

"No, just you and me, Emm. I didn't know what we should do and the more I thought about it, the more I thought that it should be just you and me."

"But what about her work friends and the people at her yoga class and stuff? What about Auntie?"

"I called your Aunt to tell her about mom and she hasn't called me back."

"I think she's on a cruise or something, I remember something about her taking a vacation, I think. She's going to be so upset when she finds out that mom is dead and that she missed the funeral."

"There's not much we can do about that Emm. I tried, that's all I can do."

Emmie nods and I'm not sure what else to say. Did I make the right choice? Should I have invited Gayle's work colleagues and friends? I didn't know them. How would I have contacted them? I didn't put the announcement of Gayle's passing in the paper because I don't know how many people read the paper anymore, besides, the funeral home said that Gayle's obituary would be online on their site. I guess people could find it that way, but I'm not sure how many people browse funeral home directories for death announcements, seems pretty morbid to me if they did.

"Dr. Cass," the funeral director says as she grasps my hand and shakes it, "I'm so sorry for your loss."

"Thank you. This is my daughter…our daughter, Emmie." I say.

"Emmie, I'm sorry for your loss. I know this must be so difficult for both of you," she says.

"Thank you," Emmie says.

"Shall we get started?" the woman asks.

"Yes."

"Please follow me this way."

She ushers us to the front of the chapel where Emmie and I sit beside each other. The urn that holds Gayle sits on a table that is surrounded by flowers.

"We're here today to celebrate the life of Gayle Cass. She was a mother, a wife, a sister, and a friend to many. She changed the lives around her as a teacher and never failed to make an impact on those she came in contact with."

*

"The service was really nice. Mom would have been happy with it."

"It was. They did a good job. Sorry that I didn't get up to say a few words, I didn't want to start crying again and I'm not the best at knowing what to say."

"It's ok. I couldn't either. I think mom knows what's on our hearts. She knows what we wanted to say."

"That's beautiful, Emm, I agree."

I found peace in her statement of Gayle knowing what's on our hearts. She has to know how sorry I am for everything and that if I could take it all back and be the man and husband that she needed me to be, I would without question. We could have had a completely different life together if I had made better choices, but there's nothing I can do about that now. The past is the past and I have to accept the fact that I'll never be able to tell her that I love her or that I'm sorry for everything. It's too late for sorry and I'll never forgive myself for how I've hurt her and for all the damage I've caused.

*

"I can't sleep; it looks like you have the same problem," Emmie says as she pulls up a stool across from me at the kitchen island.

"Yeah, I've been up for a while wandering around, thinking about things. What's on your mind…I mean other than mom? Or maybe you want to talk about that too."

"I keep thinking about what you said about me moving back home…"

My heart flutters with the hope that she's accepted my offer.

"And what did you decide?"

"I think we should talk about this over ice cream like we did when I was a little girl," Emmie smiles as she gets up from the stool and grabs bowls and spoons as I get the ice cream from the freezer.

"Cookie dough or brownie?" I ask holding up both cartons.

"Both," she says.

"Uh oh. That's certainly an indicator of a tough conversation that's about to happen," I say playfully, but she doesn't crack a smile.

Now I'm worried about what she's going to say. I want my kid home with me more than anything in the world right now and part of my soul will be ripped out if she doesn't come home to stay.

She fusses with the bowls and puts one scoop of each ice cream into our bowls.

"Cheers," she says as we clink spoons and dig in.

"Emm, what do you want to tell me? Be totally honest."

"I want to tell you that I really love New York. I love everything about it."

"New York is one of those cities that you can never forget, I agree."

"I love it so much that I see myself living there for a long time."

"Well, you've got a few years there while you go through school," I say quietly.

"What I'm trying to say is, I want to stay there, Dad. New York is going to be my home…permanently."

I put down the spoon I was stirring my ice cream with.

"Sweetie, there are so many places in the world that you have left to explore! Don't you want to see what else is out there? There are cities you haven't been to yet that may capture your heart and imagination just the same…"

"No, Dad. There is only *one* New York city."

"I understand that, Emm. I just think that you're rushing into things, you don't have to decide right now what you want for the rest of your life; you've got tons of time and I think you should finish school and then decide where you want to live."

"Dad, you're not understanding. I can't live here."

"In California?"

"No. In this house…with all the memories of mom. It hurts too much."

I feel like crying, but I stop myself as not to upset her.

"I know just how you feel," I say. "Please think about what I've said. Don't make a decision just yet give it some time."

"I want you to come and visit for Christmas."

"Instead of you coming here?"

"Yes. Let's start a new tradition."

"I'd like that," I say, and I mean it.

"Everything's going to be ok, Dad."

"I know, Emmie. We have each other and that's what matters most. Let's get some sleep, I've got to get you back to the airport in the morning so that you can get back to your studies."

"Ok, I'll see you in the morning."

This time she kisses me on the forehead, and I smile. I feel like the tables are turning and she's becoming an adult so quickly. Maybe this is how elderly parents feel when their children choose their retirement homes for them or scold them for not wearing a jacket or forgetting their bank card number. It's a weird feeling, that's for sure. I watch her leave the room before I put away the ice cream. I'm blessed to have such a good kid.

*

"Do you have enough money?"

"Yes, I have the credit card, remember?"

"Yes. Don't go crazy and max it out on shoes and concert tickets. It's supposed to be for emergencies."

"I know," Emmie says with an eyeroll.

"Do you have everything?"

"Yes, for the third time!"

"I'm just checking, I know how scatterbrained you can be."

"Gee, thanks," she says sarcastically.

"Your room is a disaster by the way. And I'm not saying a bit of a disaster, it's out of control."

"When was I supposed to have time to clean it? I've literally been here for a couple of days and didn't get a chance."

"You say that every time!"

"I know," she smiles.

"And can I reiterate how much I don't like to see your stuff scattered all over the place? Your bathroom is even worse! How that's possible, I guess I'll never know."

"Dad, it's because I need more organizational tools and more room. If I had more room, it wouldn't be so cluttered."

I smirk, "Are you kidding me? More room would just give you more opportunity to fill the space with junk."

She shakes her head and smiles, "Are you done lecturing me or are you just stalling because you don't want me to go?"

"I never want you to go, Emm. I want you to stay with me forever."

She laughs, "You sure know how to lay the guilt trip down, I guess mom taught you well."

"She did," I say.

I give Emmie a hug and then another.

"Bye, Dad. I'll see you soon ok? Remember, we have a new tradition of Christmas in New York to be excited about!"

"Yes, sweetheart. I can't wait. I'll see you soon."

I watch her go through the security gate and disappear into the crowd of people. I have an uneasy, sick feeling in the pit of my stomach, but I push it down. Seeing her again can't come soon enough.

12

I finally get the phone call that I've been dreading for a week. It is time. I'm meeting Vinnie and the boys at the abandoned warehouse just outside of the city limits as instructed. The place used to be a manufacturing plant back in the eighties; it's been empty for a long time and Vinnie purchased it around five years ago. He's sitting on the land, hoping that a developer will buy him out, but I can't see that happening anytime soon.

I feel sick to the pit of my stomach because I don't know what to expect or what's going to happen after this; the only thing that I know for sure is that I have to kill a man tonight because if I don't, it will be me who gets killed instead. I turn onto the road and shut off my headlights before I pull into the parking lot. The only other vehicle there is Vinnie's.

Charlie is waiting outside of the door and escorts me in. He goes back to his post when Vinnie acknowledges me.

"This is it! Are you ready?" He sounds oddly excited for a man who is about to be an accessory to another murder.

I look around. Mike and Tommy are there too; they're flanking who I assume is Tony Capelli's son-in-law, Joe. I can't be sure because his face is covered by a bag. Whoever it is, is sitting on a chair, restrained at the wrists, and gagged. He's wriggling around and trying to speak, but I can't make out his muffled words.

"Time to go to work! I'll let you do the honors," Vinnie says as he hands me a machete.

"You want me to use this? I don't know how to use this..." I say.

"Just think of it as a really big scalpel or whatever the fuck you use at your job," he says.

"What do you want me to do, Vin?" I ask for clarification.

"I want to you inflict as much pain on this son of a bitch as possible, while keeping him alive."

I'm starting to sweat even though the air is damp and cool.

"Vin, are you sure you want to do this?" I plead.

"Yes. This is to send the Capelli family a message that we are not to be fucked with. They take one of ours, we return the favor. The world would be a better place if people knew that whatever they did, would be done back to them."

I wipe the sweat from my forehead, "Is there anything else I can do to repay the debt I owe you?"

Vinnie raises an eyebrow, "Yeah you can give me a hundred and fifty g's."

"You know I can't do that," I say quietly.

"Then this is your last option," he says. "You understand what happens if you don't do this, right?"

"Yes."

"Just a reminder that you take his life, or I take yours. That's it, that's all," Vinnie says.

My hands are shaking so badly that I drop the machete twice.

"Jesus, Doc. I thought you guys had steady hands, they don't look too steady to me," he says.

"Sorry."

I try and regain my composure as Mike takes the bag off our victim's head; he's bleeding, and his face is badly swollen. Thank god he can't open his eyes because I don't want him looking at me while I do what I'm about to do.

I grip the machete and make the first incision on the inside of his left thigh, he screams out in pain, but the sound is muffled from the rag that's stuffed in his mouth.

"He could pass out from the pain," I say to Vinnie and I silently pray that he does.

"If that happens, oh well," Vinnie says as he takes a long drag on his cigar.

I make another incision, this time on his right arm then I move to the left thigh, being sure not to hit the major artery. Perhaps it would be more merciful of me to make him bleed out rather than take the pain that he's enduring.

I cut off his fingers one at a time. Then his toes. He's shaking and going into shock. He's going to pass out soon. Vinnie removes the gag from Tony Capelli's son-in-law's mouth, and he screams out one last time. Vinnie squeezes his cheeks until he sticks his tongue out.

"Cut out his tongue and then cut off his dick," Vinnie instructs.

He adds, "I need his heart too, Doc. That's the most important thing because I need to send it to the Capelli family."

I do as I'm told with his fingers and toes. Our victim is pale and ghost white from blood loss. He's not moving.

"Check for a pulse, Doc," Vinnie says.

"He's dead."

"Are you positive?"

"Yes," I say. I feel like throwing up or passing out, I'm not sure.

"Take out his heart."

I cut into his body and Tommy hits our victim's ribs with a sledgehammer to break them so I can get to his heart; I remove it and place it in the box that Vinnie is holding.

"Great job. You really went to town on him, it was a real work of art in my opinion," Vinnie says. "Your debt has been wiped clean, time for you to get the fuck outta here while we get rid of this guy."

I drop the machete on the dirt and head for the door.

"Burn your clothes, and your car," Vinnie instructs. "We can't have you implicated in this and we don't want to leave any ties from you to him to us. Get it?"

"Got it."

Tommy takes me around back in my car. I strip down to my underwear and throw my blood-soaked clothes into the front seat. He takes a can of gasoline and pours it over my Mercedes.

"Stand back," he says.

The gasoline ignites and I watch as the flames envelop the interior. The windows blow out from the heat and the dashboard melts. In a few minutes it's all over and burned to the ground.

"I'm supposed to drive you home now," Tommy says.

"How are Vinnie and those guys supposed to get back if we're taking their car?"

"Don't worry about that, they've got other means of transportation that will give them an alibi. Vinnie is always five steps ahead."

*

The car ride home is long and silent. I am still processing the fact that I killed a man in cold blood. As a doctor I promised to do no harm and I broke that promise tonight.

"Goodnight, Doc," Tommy says as he pulls into my driveway.

"Goodnight," I say as I shut the passenger door and run up the steps to my house.

I burst through the front door and fall to my knees. Tears rush down my face and sobs wrack my body. What have I done? Is this what my life has come to? I killed a human being tonight, my wife is dead, I have no job, and my daughter doesn't ever want to come back here. I lay on the floor of the foyer for a while and cry. What else is there for me to do? I'm a murderer, a terrible father, and I was even worse as a husband.

*

I dial Chris' number for the second time in two minutes, but it goes straight to voicemail.

"Fuck. Answer your goddamn phone!" I breathe as I end the call.

Where the fuck are you? I wonder. Chris missed the last phone call check in and I haven't heard a word from him since the last time we talked. A sick feeling fills my guts. I check my bank balance on the mobile app and see that the transfer has been automatically deposited on his end.

He's taking my money, but not giving me information about Emmie. He's broken our agreement and now I need to take action. I'm sick of this life, it's time for me to change. I have one reason for living and that's my kid. I need to get my shit together and turn over a new leaf; no more drinking or screwing around, no more lying, I need to find a new job, and I want to be closer to my daughter.

I try his number, again, straight to voicemail. I want to throw my phone against the wall, but I don't. I debate on whether to call Vinnie, but I decide against it. I don't want to have anything to do with those guys anymore. I can't if I want to change my life for the better and that's what I want so desperately, more than anything. I feel like a caged animal. What are my options? I ask myself as I pull the credit card from my wallet.

13

I don't know what the fuck is going on in New York, but I'm going to find out. As soon as I get my hands on the Chris, I'm going to kill him. I knew I shouldn't have trusted him. How the hell am I going to find this guy? I don't even know what he looks like. I pace as I dial Emmie's number. The phone rings six times before she finally answers.

"Hello?"

"Why aren't you in class?" I check my watch.

"We're on break, Dad. Why do you always think the worst?"

"Sweetheart, it's my job as your father to make sure you're on the straight and narrow, to make sure that you're going to class and not wasting my money."

"I am."

"Wasting my money or going to class?"

I can practically hear her eyes roll to the back of her head.

"Going to class, Dad."

"I'm coming early to visit. I know we have plans for Christmas, but I think a couple of days beforehand would be nice for us to do some shopping and catch up."

"When?"

"My flight leaves this afternoon, so I'll be there in time for dinner."

There's silence for a beat and I say, "Don't be so excited, Emm." Now it's my turn to roll my eyes.

"I'll meet you at the airport, JFK or LaGuardia? What's your flight number?" She says.

"Sweetheart, is everything ok with you?"

"Yeah, I'm just…"

"You're just what?"

"I'm just tired, that's all. School has taken a lot out of me."

"So, you're sure you're ok?" Another pause.

"Yes."

"But you would tell me if you weren't, right?"

"YES! Which airport and what's the flight number?" she repeats.

"JFK, flight number DL4913," I say as I find the information on my phone. "Watch for delays, you guys are supposed to be getting a lot of snow."

"Yeah, I heard that too. Ok, I'll watch for any changes. See you tonight…Dad?"

"Yes, sweetheart?"

"I miss you."

"I miss you too, baby. I love you and I'll see you soon."

"See you soon."

I grab my wallet and suitcase and get into the car that's waiting to take me to the airport.

ABOUT THE AUTHOR

L.L. Colling was born in Hamilton, Ontario, Canada. This is her second thriller, a prequel to her first titled, Obsessed with Her. In her free time, she enjoys running, traveling the world, baseball, hockey, and spending time with her best friends.

www.pandamoniumpublishing.com

Look for the second book titled, Obsessed with Her, as a follow up to this one!

Made in the USA
Monee, IL
18 August 2021